All I saw nex[...]
the cookie, s[...]
and lifting ou[...]

"Here," she snapped, holding out the cookie's fortune between two lacquered nails.

Smiling, I shook my head, took the fortune, and looked down.

"Well?" she asked.

I felt my smile collapse and the blood drain from my face.

Concerned, Sue Jan asked, "Ita, what is it?"

Tears brimming, I cried as I read,

> *"Your father was murdered. A man in*
> *a Stetson will tell you more tomorrow."*

Don't miss out on any of our great mysteries. Contact us at the following address for information on our newest releases and club information:

Heartsong Presents—MYSTERIES! Readers' Service
PO Box 721
Uhrichsville, OH 44683
Web site: www.heartsongmysteries.com

Or for faster action, call 1-740-922-7280.

Misfortune Cookies

A When the Fat Ladies Sing Mystery

Linda P. Kozar

HEARTSONG
PRESENTS
MYSTERIES

Dedication:

To Jesus—my writing partner. To my dear father, Joseph M. Pedreira, who left a trail of smiles wherever he went. To "Dootsey," my sweet mum. To my precious husband, Michael, and daughters, Katie and Lauren. To my dear friends Dannelle Woody and Jenny Kent, who helped me critique. Also to Janice Thompson and Words For The Journey Christian Writers Guild, South East Texas Region, for their excellent critique help. Also to Marian Merritt, Mignon Murrell, Denise McEwan, Kathy Burnett, Janice Thompson, and Words for the Journey Christian Writers Guild for thier excellent critique help. And special thanks to my editor, Susan Downs, who took a chance on a green mystery writer, and my copy editors, Candice and Donna, for extracting "the precious from the vile" (Jeremiah 15:19).

ISBN 978-1-59789-929-1

Cover design: Kirk DouPonce, DogEared Design
Cover Illustration: Jody Williams

Our mission is to publish and distribute inspirational products offering exceptional value and biblical encouragement to the masses.

Printed in the U.S.A.

1

WONTON FUN

You might as well know that Sue Jan and I are fat. I don't know which one of us is fatter, but we wear the same size clothes. Not that I would ever wear anything of Sue Jan's. She's way too flashy for my taste. For instance, yesterday she dyed her hair "Crazy Cherry Red" with yam undertones. She's always changing her hair color with some wild concoction. Now me, I think when you're overweight you oughta groom and dress to flatter, not call attention to your size. My hair is a warm honey brown, at least that's what the bottle says, and I wear very little makeup. I dress real conservative, too; nothing bright or flashy, just ordinary regular-type clothes.

On Thursday, as usual, we were having lunch at Chun's Hong Kong Gardens. Funny, our town's got almost one of every important thing—a bank, grocery store, diner, one-chair barbershop, pool hall, doctor's office, beauty shop/boutique, and a handful of other stores. But for some reason, we have two Chinese restaurants: Chun's Hong Kong Gardens and Cheng's Dragon Inn. There's a Wal-Mart twenty miles away in Bentley. I guess you're not really on the map unless you have one. And we don't.

I inherited a passion for Chinese food from my

father, a frequent customer of Chun's and Cheng's. But since I was on a diet—again—I ordered a bowl of egg drop soup. Unlike me, Sue Jan studied the menu like she was trying to decipher the Rosetta stone.

She eyed our waiter. "Tan, you got anything new on the pupu platter this week?"

He offered a polite bow. "No, we do not, MizSue-Jan, but I could make one up special for you."

"Oooh." She flashed a red-lipped smile. "I'd like that a lot."

"Okay then, what can I get for you, MizSueJan?"

Without looking back at the menu, she rattled off, "Some crabmeat sticks, those cute tiny egg rolls, shrimp toast, fried wontons, barbeque beef, spareribs, and fan-tailed shrimp with extra pepper on 'em, if you don't mind. And since Lovita ordered the egg drop, I'm gonna want the silky corn crabmeat soup. Got that?"

His pen flew across the pad, trying to catch up, but then, no waiter has ever been able to keep up with her.

"Sue Jan, you need to slow down or Tan's gonna need a course in stenography. Besides, why'd you order all that for an appetizer?"

She swirled her hand over the table as Tan walked off to fill our orders. "It's for both of us, girlfriend."

"But you know I'm on a diet."

She pointed a red-clawed finger at me. "Lovita Horton, don't you go and lose weight. Skinny women get all wrinkly in the face." Sue Jan somehow managed to suck in her cheeks and scrunch her face, her impression of a typical skinny woman. "You never see wrinkles on a balloon, do you?"

"Nooo." I snickered, barely able to swallow a sip of iced tea.

"So that settles it." She pounded the table. "We're sharing lunch."

Just then, Tan returned with our soup. "The pupu platter will be out in a few minutes. You ladies ready to order the main course?"

"Tan, we're sharing today." Sue Jan winked and lowered her voice to her idea of a whisper. "Lovita's trying to lose weight."

He looked confused, but he nodded, trying to be polite. He cast a glance my way from the corner of his eye.

I glared at her, but Sue Jan knew better than to look up just then. "Sooo, we'll have a large order of shrimp-fried rice to go with the regular sticky rice with our main course. And let's just order Lovita's favorite dish, why don't we." She looked up at me, lashes fanning, her face masked with a faux look of innocent intent. "What was that thing you used to order all the time?"

"Shrimp egg foo yong," I grumbled. She knew me too well. I loved that dish, but mostly because it was my daddy's favorite. Tan took it off the menu a long time ago. *Right after Daddy di—*

"That's right." She thrust the menu at Tan. "Lovita and I are gonna share the shrimp egg foo yong. I know you won't mind making that up special for her, and while you're at it, we might as well have something else, too. Hmm."

I tapped the table to get her attention. "I thought you said we were sharing?" Just to spite her I added,

"Well, instead of shrimp egg foo yong, I would prefer to have the triple dee-light."

Her teaspoon hovered in midair for a moment. "Really?" She blinked the surprise away. "Suit yourself, girl. Anywho, I thought we should order two entrées because then we'll have leftovers to share for din-din." She tapped her temple with her index finger. "I'm always thinking, my friend, always thinking.

"Okay, so Lovita will have the triple dee-light and"—she pointed at Tan—"I think I'll have the kung pao chicken."

Tan and I gasped. We both knew that Sue Jan hated the kung pao chicken. She said she felt compelled to order it from time to time though, hoping that Chef Hans Han might finally "get it right." But I knew, we all knew, she had ulterior motives.

In no time flat we polished off the soup, followed by the pupu platter. Then our triple dee-light and the kung pao chicken arrived on steaming-hot plates. I watched her through a few tentative chews, waiting for what I knew would happen next.

After a few halfhearted bites, she threw down her fork. "Now what do you expect," she shouted, nostrils flaring, "from a German-Chinese chef?"

I shrugged my shoulders. "Szechwan schnitzel?"

She couldn't catch her breath and when she finally did, she snorted out laughs in short spurts. A couple of bean sprouts hung off the side of her mouth. I pointed at her, laughing.

"Sue Jan, wipe those bean sprouts off you." I couldn't help but sneer. "After all, you wouldn't want

Chef Hans to see you like that."

She looked up. Panicked, eyes wide, she gulped. "He's not out here, is he? Just the mention of his name gives me chill bumps." With one deft motion, she swiped the bean sprouts from her face into the air.

Not wanting to know where the sprouts landed, I looked straight ahead. "No," I answered between bites of my triple delight. "Your honey Hans ain't left the kitchen yet." Not that Hans was in Chun's kitchen most of the time. Hans was the master chef at his mother's restaurant, Cheng's, but a couple days a week, he worked for his uncle, who allowed him to do what Mama Loo didn't—experiment with recipes.

Most of Sue Jan's attempts at snagging a man were unsuccessful. But you had to hand it to her for trying. Not like me. After a few rejections I just sorta gave up on ever finding the man of my dreams—or any man for that matter. I figured if God wanted me to jump over the broom, He was gonna have to get me the groom.

Sue Jan suddenly slapped her sequined, suitcase-sized purse onto the table and started digging. First her hand disappeared, then her arm to the elbow.

"Girl, you looking for some lipstick or performing psychic surgery?"

"Very funny," Sue Jan said with a smirk. "I need some lipstick. You got some?"

Just as I was reaching for my much smaller purse, she exclaimed loudly, "Oh, wait, I found it!" To her surprise, she pulled out a battery-operated nose hair trimmer instead. I bit my lip, reached for my purse again, rooted around fast as I could, and handed her my lipstick.

" 'Candied Apple,' " she voiced, doubtful. "Hmm, I suppose that'll do. Uh, thanks, Ita." Momentarily distracted, she left the patented Trim Schnoz right next to her unused chopsticks.

Which was just like something Sue Jan would do. She and I are best friends. Ever since elementary school, we've lived in the same place all our lives—Wachita. We pronounce it "Waah-chee-tah," with the emphasis on the *tah*. It's from an Indian word that means "place of stagnant waters," which suits this town just right. Sometimes, living in a small town feels like you're sitting in a puddle of stagnant water, not going anywhere, not making your mark in life. Other times, though, it feels good, like wearing an old, comfortable pair of shoes. I love it here and I hate it here. It's that kind of place.

"Do you think he'll come out of the kitchen?" Sue Jan was anxious, her eyes on the swinging doors.

"He will if you complain again."

Just then, Tan showed up at the table with a stainless pitcher sheathed in frost, to refill our glasses. Unlike other restaurants, Tan made sure his iced tea was Eskimo-cold. And on a hot day, there was nothing better.

"Evee-ting okay, ladies?"

"Be nice," I whispered to Sue Jan.

Tan was a pleasant and patient man. Short and efficient, his hair dulled by gray and thin on top, he always forced a nervous smile in the presence of Sue Jan, and today was no exception. He looked down at the table, his eyes focused for a moment on the Trim Schnoz. A puzzled (or was it horrified?) look washed across his face and he looked away.

"Tan?" I discreetly covered the trimmer with my dinner napkin.

"Yes?" He smiled, relieved to focus on me.

"My triple delight was dee-lightful and dee-lishus. Chef Hans has really outdone himself today. You tell him that, okay?"

He nodded, smiling. "Yes, yes, I will."

A booming voice, peppered with West Texas twang, broke in. "Well, you can tell Chef Hans a thing or two from me, *too*."

Hesitant, he turned to Sue Jan and bowed halfway. "What can I tell him for you, MizSueJan?"

It was my turn to interrupt. "You can tell Chef Hans that she's crazy in love with him." A handful of sticky rice plastered my face almost before I finished talking.

"Don't listen to her, she, she's—" Sue Jan's face flushed red. "You just tell him that he still doesn't know how to make kung pao chicken right. It tasted like kung pao Kibbles 'n Bits!"

"Sue Jan!" I cried out, annoyed as I picked rice off my face. "That was mean."

She threw her head to the side and flipped her hair in dramatic defiance. "Sorry about the rice."

"You know full well I'm not talking about the rice."

"Well, it did taste bad," she snipped, then she stuck her tongue out at me.

Tan's eyes were looking away, toward the safety of

the swinging doors to the kitchen. He looked as if he wanted to bolt. "So sorry, MizSueJan. Let me bring you some-ting else."

"No." She shook her head. "I don't want anything else, Tan."

"Do you want a refund, MizSueJan?"

She sighed and picked at some imaginary lint on her fuchsia blouse. "Noooooo."

I slammed my hands down on the table. "Cut to it. Tell him you want to see the chef."

Relieved, Tan bowed, picked up the hem of his apron, and wiped it across his brow. "I will retrieve him for you, MizSueJan." He burst through the swinging doors and disappeared.

I turned back to her. "Well, now you've done it. Any second now, a very angry blue-eyed German-Chinese man is gonna bust through that door with a butcher's knife in his hand."

Sue Jan sat up straight and perky. "How's my lipstick look?"

I let out a tired little sigh and muttered, "Just like mine."

2

THE CORNSTARCH THICKENS

Chef Hans Han stood over us, all six foot two of him. I glanced at his hands and thought it strange that a large man would have such tiny hands. No butcher's knife in sight, though. Not even a paring knife.

I looked across the table at Sue Jan. After a hasty trip to the ladies' room, she'd returned with the flame of "Crazy Cherry Red" hair swept back in an attractive updo, eyes lined a metallic blue, brows penciled in brownish-black, and my "Candied Apple" red lip color slathered across her wide mouth. Glittery purple gem-stone hoops hung from her ears, completing whatever look she was going for.

"Hellooo, Hans," she purred, oozing with flirt-atious expectation. Her neck tilted backward, and she stared up at him, real dreamy-like. Her masculine ideal had small ice-blue eyes, whitish eyelashes, and a carved-statue face. The only parts on him that showed a dip in the Asian gene pool were his sleek black hair and tiny hands. Not a fat cell anywhere on his body either.

Chef Hans clicked his boots together like a military man and bowed forward. "Miz Sue Jan." He kissed her hand and, for a moment, Sue Jan was completely speechless. No one, to my knowledge, had ever had that effect on her, not even when she won a twenty-five-dollar gift certificate to Brandee's Catfish Kitchen in a radio contest two weeks ago and Crazy Lenny Z, her favorite DJ, presented it to her.

Before she could catch her breath, Chef Hans turned to me. "Miz Lovita." He gripped my left hand in his and kissed it. His lips felt dry. For some reason, I don't know why, I felt like pulling my hand away.

Turning back to Sue Jan, he spoke, "Mr. Tan has informed me that you are unhappy with the kung pao chicken entrée you ordered." He forced out a quick laugh. "He told me that you made some disparaging remarks about my prowess as a chef. I can assure you, I have been fully trained in the art of Asian cooking. In fact, I have two culinary degrees." He slowly shook his head and wagged his finger while making a *tic-tic-tic* sound. Resting his baby doll hands on the end of the table, he leaned in toward Sue Jan.

I gasped as Hans loomed over our table.

His thin lips cracked upward a sliver. His attempt at a smile, I guessed. "Other customers rave about my special recipe for kung pao. In fact, a reporter at the *Bentley Buzzard* recently gave us a favorable review." He leaned in farther, now face-to-face with her. "Now, Miz Sue Jan, please tell me why you are so unhappy with my dish."

Obviously infatuated, and overcome by his presence, Sue Jan gulped as the color drained from her face. "Well. . .ah. . .ah. . ." Her eyes seemed to roll like blue and white marbles to the left and to the right. The muscle on her right eye started jumping. "It—it was

Lovita's idea that I should complain."

My jaw dipped down and up like a fish caught on a hook. She shot me a menacing look; an expression so desperate that I just shut my mouth and tilted my head to the side in amazement.

"You see, she thinks that I," she snorted out, "I mean me, I mean I, personally, make the best kung pao chicken there is and that since I do, maybe you should come over for dinner one night." She smiled at him and blinked a couple of times for effect, then she looked my way, begging me with her eyes to cover the lie.

The *statue* turned to me. "Is this true, Miz Lovita?"

Now I personally believe that lying's a sin, but the Ten Commandments are like "Hints from Heloise" to Sue Jan. We're roommates, so I know firsthand that she pretty much worships St. Mattress on Sundays. Sometimes though, when she buys a new hat or a new outfit and wants to show it off, she'll come to church with me.

So, in frantic response to Chef Hans's question, I grabbed my glass of iced tea and gulped as if I could dive in and swim away. That's when I gasped. A piece of ice stuck in my throat. I stood up, pointing to my neck. I felt like my eyes were bulging out of my face.

I heard Sue Jan yelling, "Don't just stand there Hans—help her!" But it sounded distant and distorted, like the audio in a film running in slow motion.

Everything around me seemed to be turning white. Suddenly, two arms enveloped me from behind and jabbed my midsection. The cube shot out and bounced off the table like a piece of hail. I collapsed into my chair. Sue Jan simultaneously fanned my face and handed me a glass of water. I closed my eyes and took in a few deep breaths before I dared open them again.

"Thank you, Hans. I think you saved my life."

"Hans?" exclaimed Sue Jan. "He didn't save your life, someone else did. I'm real disappointed in Hans. He can't even perform the Heimlich maneuver. Ain't that a German word? Heimlich? And he couldn't even do it. He ran off to the kitchen, but he's still cute. . . ."

I felt a tap my shoulder. I opened my eyes and looked behind me. The arms that had somehow made it around my waist belonged to Monroe Madsen. Good ole Monroe. I managed a faint smile and looked him in the eye. "Thanks for saving my life," I rasped. "What are you doing here, Monroe? I haven't seen you for about four, maybe five years."

"I've been here all along, here in the restaurant, today, that is. Just a table away, but there's a big bamboo plant in between, so I guess we couldn't see one another." He paused. "I could sure hear you all though."

"I'll bet you could, Monroe." I snickered, then coughed. I was definitely not ready to snicker. I tossed my hair back from my face. Choking on that cube had left me all askew. "Last I heard, you graduated with a law degree."

"That's right. I worked over in Houston for a while, but now I'm back. I was just hired at a firm over in Bentley." Monroe pushed his round brown glasses back up on the bridge of his nose where they belonged.

Monroe was a classmate of ours. A real nerd. He'd carried a big torch for Sue Jan back then, but she never paid him any mind.

"Why don't you join us, Monroe?" I invited.

"Oh, a. . .Monroe"—Sue Jan pursed her lips, staring at his chest—"let me help you with that."

"What?" Monroe and I both asked. *Why is she being so nice to him?*

It was obvious where the bean sprouts had landed. Sue Jan dipped her napkin in a glass of ice water and wrung it out.

"Sorry about that." She brushed the sprouts off, scowled at the stain left behind on his suit, and dabbed at it. Then she beamed a tentative smile his way. "You finished eating?"

Before he could open his mouth to answer, Tan, ever vigilant, delivered to our table Monroe's plate, cutlery, and a fresh napkin.

Monroe's eyes lit up. He stuttered a thank-you, his gaze all the while on Sue Jan, and finally answered my question. "Y–yes, I do believe I would like to join you."

"There," Sue Jan announced with a pat to the soggy spot on his chest. "You're good as new."

He melted into a chair at our table.

I looked him over. Monroe was wearing his usual play clothes—a wrinkled blue and white seersucker suit and a baseball cap. *Some things never change.*

"I'm looking for a house here in Wachita," he

announced. "Right now I'm staying with my sister in Bentley, but I—I'm kinda partial to this town."

"You're moving back *here*?" I asked, surprised.

"Monroe," belted out Sue Jan, "I want to thank you for saving Lovita Loco. But seriously, why *are* you moving back here? Bentley's bigger and that's where the firm is, too. Everybody else is trying to get out of this town, and you're moving back?"

His face flushed red. "Th—th—hank you, Sue Jan. I guess I'm m—moving back for a variety of reasons. Um, I guess you could say, 'there's no place like home.'"

I raised an eyebrow, my mind still a few sentences behind. "'Loco?' I guess I should be grateful that you can't call me Lovita the Liar instead. I cannot believe you fibbed and expected me to. . ."

Just then, Hans and Tan ran out of the kitchen, speaking rapid-fire Chinese with what sounded like a bit of German thrown in, which stopped abruptly when they reached the table.

"You okay, MizLovita?" asked Tan, his brow furrowed with concern.

"I'm fine, Tan." I answered. "Thanks to Monroe here," I said, pointing.

Tan threw his arms up with dramatic flair. "All your lunches—on the house."

"No, Tan," I insisted. "We've been enough trouble today. We're paying."

He shook his hands together as if in urgent prayer. "Please, MizLovita, accept this complimentary lunch, and we will have no more trouble between us."

"You heard the man, Lovita!" boomed Sue Jan.

"Don't be rude."

"No, Tan, I insist we pay. Fair is fair." Then I turned my attention back to Sue Jan. "Rude?" I screeched, my voice still a bit scratchy. "You think *I'm* rude?"

Sue Jan smiled at Tan. "Thank you so much for making our dining experience here at Chun's Hong Kong Gardens so enjoyable. Now, would you please bring us our fortune cookies?" She mimicked Hans's earlier move and tick-tocked her index finger like a pendulum. "After all, the din-din's not over until the cookie crumbles. Oh, and one for Monroe, too, please." Sue Jan, in all her glory, turned to Monroe and smiled.

Now I can't be certain, but I believe I saw the whites in Tan's wide-opened eyes before he scurried off to the kitchen to fetch some fortune cookies.

. Chef Hans Han was halfway to the kitchen himself when Sue Jan hollered at him. "I'm not mad at you any more, Hans! In fact, I'll expect you for dinner on Sunday night at 6:30 sharp, okay?"

He stopped short and pivoted around kinda slow. But before he could make an excuse, she went in for the kill. "That's still your day off, isn't it?"

I had to hand it to her. She always did her dating homework.

His shoulders bowed inward. "Yes, Miz Sue Jan."

Monroe's shoulders caved, too, but Sue Jan wasn't looking at him.

He still likes her. Even after all these years. She's the real reason he's moving back here.

"Drop the *Miz*, will ya? Call me Sue Jan or just call

me, if you know what I mean." She winked.

When the swinging door of the kitchen opened, I saw the blur of someone handing something to Tan as he strode out toward the dining area. In a blink, the door swung shut.

Tan and Hans paused to exchange looks, then they passed each other. The cookies were arranged on three little black trays on top of the bills and placed in front of each of us. My tray had a red pen on it, decorated with lotus blossoms. We thanked Tan again. He bowed and made a beeline for the kitchen.

Monroe reached for the bills. "Ladies, now it's my turn to insist."

Sue Jan and I looked at one another. She shrugged. "Thanks."

"Yes, thanks. That's so nice of you."

Cheeks red with excitement, Sue Jan scrubbed her palms together and looked over at Monroe. "Get ready to open your fortune cookie. I'm feeling lucky."

He sat up straight. Sue Jan dealt the cookies off the trays like cards and, with one swift blow of her fist, crushed her cookie to smithereens right in the wrapper. She ripped it open and pulled out the tiny slip of rice paper.

> *"When dark clouds gather,*
> *your answers will rain down."*

She looked up, disappointed. "Now what is that supposed to mean?"

Monroe braved an explanation. "Maybe when

there's a storm, you'll find the answers to some questions you have. I looked at the Weather Channel before I came here today, and they say we're in for a real cats-and-dogs soaker tomorrow, maybe even tornadoes."

Sue Jan stared ahead, then she squinted her eyes in thought. "Maybe," she mouthed almost inaudibly. She looked at me. "What do you think, girl?"

"Answers are a whole lot better than cats and dogs falling on you," I said.

Sue Jan busted into giggles. "You always have a snippy little something to say, Ita. Now cut the chatter and open yours up. I'm dying to hear what your cookie has to say."

"Not me, Sue Jan," I insisted. "Monroe is next. We're going clockwise."

"Oh, all right. Go ahead, Monroe!" she barked. Monroe fumbled with the wrapper and, in the process, heaved a heavy but quiet belch. I could tell that it hurt him to keep it inside, but Monroe was ever the gentleman. Sue Jan squinched her nose in disgust, but she didn't say anything.

"True love is only a heartbeat away."

When he finished reading it, Monroe looked up straight in Sue Jan's face. That's when I knew for sure that he still liked her, maybe even loved her.

Sue Jan was livid. "Now why didn't I get that one? I think Monroe got my cookie and I got his. Let's trade," she ordered. Before he could react, she grabbed the fortune from his hand and thrust hers into his.

"Uh-uh, no fair trading fortunes. What you got is what you git. Give it back," I ordered.

"But Lovita," Sue Jan whinnied like a pitiful pony.

"Give it back," I repeated.

Though reluctant, she exchanged papers with him.

"Sue Jan, I don't mind."

"Uh-uh, Monroe," I cautioned, holding up my index finger.

Sue Jan looked at me. "Okay, Miz Fortune Cookie Police, open yours."

I smiled and decided to drive her a little further over the edge. I crinkled the wrapper, like I was trying to get it off but couldn't. "They just make these wrappers impossible to open. . . .Wait. . . .Think I'm getting it. . . .No."

All I saw next was a flash of red claws grabbing the cookie, smashing it, ripping the wrapper off, and lifting out the tiny white paper.

"Here," she snapped, holding out the cookie's fortune between two lacquered nails.

Smiling, I shook my head, took the fortune, and looked down.

"Well?" she asked.

I felt my smile collapse and the blood drain from my face.

Concerned, Sue Jan asked, "Ita, what is it?"

Tears brimming, I cried as I read,

*"Your father was murdered. A man in
a Stetson will tell you more tomorrow."*

3

TEXAS TORNADOES, TOMATILLOS, AND A TEN-GALLON HAT

A ray of morning sunlight filtered through the show window of Lovita's Cut 'n Strut, highlighting swirling galaxies of dust. The beam ended in a canister of blue sanitizing liquid, refracting a psychedelic splash on the wall.

I inherited the shop from my mama, Bessie Mae Horton. My daddy, Clark W. Horton, a Texas Ranger, died from heart problems when I was just sixteen. Right at the kitchen table. He had just started on his bacon and eggs when he was called. He was gone before the toast popped up. I'll always miss him.

Mama lived fifteen years longer than Daddy, and I still ache to hear her sweet voice. When I wake up in the morning, sometimes I can swear I smell her homemade buttery biscuits in the oven.

Anyway, before my mama died, she had a special ceremony and ribbon cutting for the shop she renamed Lovita's Cut 'n Strut. She had a new sign made, too. It's faded out a bit now, but I don't have the heart to replace it.

In a quiet mood, because of yesterday's ominous fortune cookie message, I unpacked a new shipment of clothes for the boutique part of the store. Prom dresses. The season was fast approaching, and I always stocked the shop for giggling girls and their mamas to buy their first glamorous dresses. Tiaras, glittery jewelry, even shoes and tiny sparkly purses completed my part of the fantasy. I held up an ornate tiara to admire it.

The rest was up to Sue Jan for the hair and Bo, our nail specialist, for the mani- and pedicures. Unless, of course, we got busy. Not that I was bad at curling and pinning the updos. My mama taught me to do that and I had a gift for it, the one and only styling gift I inherited.

Like I said, Bo, Tan's daughter, does the nails in the salon part-time till 3:00 every day, then she goes to work at the restaurant until late at night. She's almost nineteen and real good with manis and pedis, but super quiet. Sue Jan hates dead air, so she makes up for the quiet. I don't think she ever stops talking.

My thoughts were elsewhere today, though. I just couldn't get that fortune cookie fortune out of my head. What did that message mean? I knew full well how my father died. After all, I was there. Maybe the message was some sort of mean prank. Could someone be that heartless? And if so, why?

As if reading my thoughts, Sue Jan pointed her rattail comb at me. "I don't know why you're so upset, Lovita." Sue Jan popped her gum, fingers nimbly unrolling Lula Mae's frayed silk curls.

"What? What?" asked Miz Lula, bobbing her cotton-top head.

Sue Jan patted her shoulder. "Not you, Miz Lula.

I was talking to Lovita over there." She pointed at me and, ever the multitasker, stuck out her tongue.

Miz Lula smiled, then answered, somewhere above a whisper, "Oh, okay." She pulled out a used tissue from her sleeve, blew her nose, then tucked the soiled hankie back in.

Sue Jan shifted her eyes and tapped her right foot, telltale signs she was impatient to finish. "Anyway, Lovita, that fortune cookie fortune had to be some sort of sick joke and when I find out who did it"—she pointed a curler menacingly—"I'm gonna put on my pointy-toed shoes and. . ."

A snore erupted from Miz Lula's mouth, now resting on her shoulder.

"What about the hat?" I asked. "And who do you think put that message in my fortune cookie? Tan denied that he or Hans Han had anything to do with it."

"What about the hat? How many men in Texas wear cowboy hats? It could be just 'bout anybody 'round here. Plus, Tan looked plenty surprised when he saw the fortune. I don't think he knew anything about it."

"I called the sheriff's office in Bentley this morning to report it, and the operator said they'd be sending someone over soon to investigate."

"Really?" Sue Jan asked. "When did you do that?"

"This morning when you were hogging the bathroom." I sighed.

I shook my head. "Tan told us that he and Hans Han were the only two working that day. But I could have sworn I saw someone else in the kitchen, for just a flash of a second, mind you. Do you think they would lie?"

"Maybe Greta was in the kitchen, scraping plates or making up a batch of that secret duck sauce or something."

"Well, you would think a man would remember if his wife was in the kitchen."

Sue Jan stroked her chin in a rare philosophic moment. "If only that were true, Ita. The world would be a better place." She shook a hairbrush at me. "When Bo gets in at eleven, I'm going to ask her if she has any idea who it could have been. Ooh, that one's beautiful," she cooed.

"What?" I asked. I lifted the top dress off the armful I had brought out of the box.

"That aqua dress with the silver sequins."

I held it up for her to get a better look. Blue-green iridescent satin accented with tiny silver sequins and crystals. "Oh, yeah, Sue Jan, that's one of my favorites. That's why I bought it at the wholesalers market last month. I figured I wouldn't have any trouble selling it."

"Tell me, Ita, does it come in a bodaciously big-beautiful-woman size?"

"I don't know, but I'll check for you. What do you want with it anyway? You planning on going to the prom?" I teased.

"You never know what fa-fa she-she event a date might ask me to go to." She winked. "Oh, and I want a tiara, too."

"A tiara?" *She's got to be kidding.*

Just then, *ting-a-ling*, the door opened, and a gust

of wind blew papers and snippets of cut hair all over the place.

Bo struggled to shut the door as Sue Jan picked a delicate swatch of Miz Lula's white hair off her lips.

I laughed. "Your lip gloss is like flypaper, Sue Jan." She scrunched her nose back at me.

"Hi, Bo."

"Good morning, MizLovita. Good morning, Miz-SueJan," she answered with perfect politeness. Bo handed Sue Jan a brown paper bag dotted with grease stains, then she walked quietly to a mirror to comb her sleek black hair into a ponytail.

I motioned at the door. "It's a little windy out there, eh, Bo?"

"A little." She smiled.

"A little windy?" boomed Sue Jan. "You're such a teeny thing, hon. We're gonna have to tie you down in a high wind, or you'll get blown around like a dandelion."

"A little candy?" Miz Lula, resurrected by a word she thought she heard, raised her head in response. "Oh, no thanks, I'm not supposed to have any, what with my diverticulitis and all."

I stifled a laugh, and Sue Jan pretended to sneeze. She struggled the words out, "You sure, Miz Lula? Not even a little bit?"

"Bo."

"Yes, MizLovita?" Bo looked up from her nail table.

I pulled out the fortune to show her. "I got this in my fortune cookie yesterday."

She stared at the white slip of paper. "I—I do

not understand." She shook her head, her lovely brow furrowed.

Sue Jan reached over to hand the other two fortunes to her. "What about these, Bo? Ever see these? The one about the storm was mine and—and the one about love was Monroe's, but personally, I believe I was supposed to get the one about love."

A light of recognition illuminated Bo's eyes. "Yes, yes. I have seen *these* fortunes before." Seemingly confused, she switched her position in the chair to face me.

I warmed a reassuring smile her way. "Bo, can you tell me where your father gets the fortune cookies for the restaurant?"

She hesitated a moment before answering. "I believe they are from a supplier in Houston."

"Could you find out for me?" I asked, trying not to sound as desperate as I felt.

"Of course, MizLovita." She blinked. "I will speak to my father."

"And bring us a big bowl of them fortune cookies from the restaurant, Bo." Sue Jan smiled, talking over the whoosh of the blow-dryer. "Lovita and I can investigate and see if there's any more weird messages. I'll sacrifice my figure to get to the bottom of things."

"More like the bottom of the bowl," I answered, hands on my hips. *Not a bad idea, though.*

Ring. Ring. Without looking up from primping Miz Lula's hair, Sue Jan grabbed for the phone with her free hand but bonked herself on the ear with the now-silent blow-dryer instead. "Ouch!" *Ring.*

I giggled, though I knew I shouldn't.

Frown lines on her forehead, she rubbed at her ear and answered as pleasant as she could muster under the circumstances. "Lovita's Cut 'n Strut, we tease to please. Oh, okay, sure, we'll have her ready for you in just a minute. I'm almost done." She hung up the phone.

She swiveled Miz Lula around to face her. "Miz Lula," she said, voice exaggerated and extra loud, "that's your daughter Rose calling from her cell phone. She's coming by to pick you up now. She's worried about the weather going bad. All you need is a spritz and a spray and, wah-lah, you'll be done. Okay?"

Three minutes later, Miz Rose and Miz Lula were on their way, and another gust of wind scattered some leaves and papers and knocked over some nail polish on Bo's table. Bo and I scurried to tidy the mess, but Sue Jan sat down in a client chair and opened the take-out bag.

"Ummm. Thanks, Bo. I'm so hungry. Ya'll are welcome to have some of this."

"What is it?"

"It's from Tejania Taqueria," she crunched. "How much do I owe you, Bo?"

Bo leaned in, using a pen with red ink, to scribble the amount on the bag.

"Thanks." She smiled side-a-ways at her. "Ita, I got some green tomatillo sauce and some nice warm tortilla chips here—the megathin kind. You want some, girls?"

"Now, just a minute. Tejania Taqueria is in Bentley; that's twenty miles from here."

Sue Jan waved a salty hand in a circle. "And your point is?"

I turned to Bo. "Did Sue Jan make you go twenty miles out of your way this morning just to get her some chips and dip?"

Bo stared down at the hairy floor. "Well, to be precise, MizLovita, I did not go out of my way much. My father had an errand for me to do."

"Regardless, Sue Jan, I can't believe how you use people to get what you want."

Hopping out of her chair in defiance, she gestured with the bag in one hand, salsa in the other. "What did I do now? Is it a crime to crave chips and dip?"

"You always have food on the brain. Y–you eat like a shrew."

"What's that supposed to mean?" she screeched, chips flying out her mouth.

"They're these little mouse-like critters that eat a lot, but they're not fat or anything. I saw this special on the Science Channel about small animals, and a shrew eats three times its own body weight every day."

"So? Are you comparing me to some kind of a rat?"

"Don't you see?" I threw up my arms in despair of ever getting her to understand. "That totally describes you, Sue Jan. You graze nonstop from sunup to sundown."

She squinted her eyes, and I knew she was about to volley in my direction. "And what about you, Lovita? You like lifting your fork as much as I do. And if you don't get some self-control they're gonna need a forklift to pick *you* up."

I pointed at her. "Oh yeah! Well, at least I *try* to

diet. I *try* to exercise sometimes, too. You know how it is. I gain weight without even *trying* to. Sometimes I just look at a piece of cheesecake and the fat demons jump on me. What's *your* excuse?"

Sue Jan pointed a finger at me and seemed about to say something but just then, a shadow fell across the beam of sunlight. I looked out the window and saw a wall of dark clouds tinged green in the distance. I walked over to the picture window, followed by Bo.

"There's some big bad clouds gathering out there, Sue Jan. Looks like your Monroe was right about what he saw on the Weather Channel."

"Lovita, he's not 'my Monroe,' and I'll thank you to not say that again or I'll have to hurt you." Sue Jan put down the bag of chips and joined us.

"What do you think?" I turned to ask. "We'd better call and cancel our appointments today, girls. I say we get down to the storm cellar in my house. Looks like those black clouds'll breed some twisters for sure."

Sue Jan's mouth hung open, and then she began mouthing something.

I waved my hand in front of her face. "Hello? Sue Jan?"

She grabbed my head in a viselike grip and turned me back to the window. "Lovita, instead of looking at those black clouds, you oughta be looking at that man across the street. Remember, 'Your father was murdered. A man in a Stetson will tell you more tomorrow.' "

4

FASHION, FUNNEL CLOUDS,
AND FUNNEL CAKES

Well, where is he? What happened to the man in the cowboy hat?" I yelled, barely audible over the rising wind whipping around us as we stood outside the shop.

"I don't see him!" she yelled back. "He just flat-out disappeared!"

"Wait!" I pointed. "Look over there. Way down the street."

"Where?" Bo asked, her silken hair lifting like a kite.

"I don't see him, Ita." Sue Jan squinted, trying to protect her eyes from the stinging dust.

I extended my arm. "There. Now he's almost to the filling station."

A man in a beige sports coat was chasing something down the street. Every time he came close to his quarry, his boot kicked it away, clumsily driving the buff blur into another blast of wind and starting the ridiculous routine all over again.

"MizLovita, it's getting dark. Maybe we should go." Bo looked concerned.

She was right. Midday and it was getting darker.

The storm was fixin' to bear down hard on little Wachita. "Let's go to my house. I know we'll be safe there."

Bo shook her head and pointed down Main Street toward Chun's Hong Kong Gardens. "No, MizLovita, I'll go to my father's restaurant."

"You sure, Bo?"

She nodded her head, turned, and ran down the street toward Chun's, dodging blown papers and leaves. After I locked up the shop, Sue Jan and I jumped in my car and sped through two red lights to get out of town. All the radio channels were on alert; there was a tornado warning. Someone in Bentley spotted funnel clouds. I started to sweat.

"Git us home, Lovita." Sue Jan leaned forward, scraping the air with her arms as if she could row us home faster.

"We're almost there, Suey." A rolled-up newspaper stung the right side of my head.

"Hey! That wasn't very nice." I glared her way for a moment then trained my eyes back on the road.

"I told you not to call me Chop Suey anymore, Ita. It ain't dignified enough for an adult, a—a *young* adult like me. Suppose Hans heard you calling me that? He's not even from here. He's from some place in Germany where men yodel."

"That's in Switzerland, *Suey*."

"What's that?" she asked, panicked and pointing at the windshield.

We looked up through the windshield at a spiky black cloud in the distance. The tip of it began to rotate in a graceful pirouette.

"Uh-oh," I gasped.

Sue Jan held my shoulder in a bear-trap grip. "We're gonna die, Ita! That's a funnel cloud, a baby tornado coming down. Then it's gonna get big and nasty and carry us away and there won't be enough left of us to pick up in a vacuum cleaner, and I'll never have my date with Hans. Never."

It was strange for it to be so dark outside in the middle of the day. I opened the car window. Seemed quiet, too. No birds singing or crickets chirping. Even the leaves in the trees were still. I screeched the car to a halt by the back door. I don't even know how we got out, but in a flash we were inside tripping over chairs, knocking over vases and dishes, and grabbing Sue Jan's four fat cats on our way down to Daddy's fallout shelter. My daddy built it under the house in the fifties, when everybody was scared of an atomic bomb going off.

I had to admit the whole setup was pretty clever. Daddy built a secret hinged shelf inside our walk-in kitchen pantry. Behind that was a stairway full of cobwebs that led down to the heavy door made of super-thick steel. Four people could live and sleep real comfortable for a couple of weeks. It was fully stocked with food. Medical supplies, too. And an air filter was supposed to protect us from breathing radioactive air. Daddy tried to think of everything.

Not many people knew about it, of course. Out in public, we called it our "storm shelter." It's not the sort of thing you're supposed to advertise. You don't want everybody showing up at your shelter door, wanting in. I know he was worried. That's why he built it, out of love for us. He didn't want me and Mama turning mutant or anything.

Once the door was closed and the air lock turned, everything was quiet except for the cats, who were meowing, all nervous-like, and looking for somewhere to hide. We were snug inside. That was certain. But we could hear little bumps and crashes and the sound of the wind howling.

The overhead industrial lights went dim all of a sudden. I had 'em set on low to conserve power, but the storm was affecting things. A quick flip of a switch fixed that.

"Hey, thanks for turning the lights up." Sue Jan turned around surveying the place, though she had visited the shelter a gazillion times before. "This is like a fifties museum. Even the shampoo and toothpaste, the combs and shaving cream are all from then." She held up a tube. "They don't even make this brand anymore." She drew in an excited breath. "You could charge admission! Why didn't I think of that before? Think of the extra bucks you could make, showing people a real live atomic-bomb shelter right here in Wachita. What do you think?"

Hands on my hips like a sugar bowl, I scrunched up my nose in disapproval. "We have a few other things to worry about right now, Sue Jan—like a tornado out there scouring through town, maybe even through this house."

I turned on the emergency radio. A siren immediately sounded. *"The towns of Wachita, Bentley, and*

*Dayton till five o'clock central standard time. . . . Warning!
. . . Warning! . . . . A tornado sighting has been confirmed
in the towns of Bentley and Wachita! . . . . Residents are
advised to take cover immediately!"*

Sue Jan reached over to switch it off.

"Hey, why'd you do that?"

"We've heard enough, Lovita. We've seen the
twister ourselves. It's probably tearing off pieces of
your house like cotton candy right now." She sniffed.
"Into itty bitty pieces. Yup."

"Thank you for that."

She sniffed again. "Well, at least we're safe. And
the kitty cats." She reached down to pet Vicki-Lou,
the fattest of the four kitties and clearly the alpha
kitty. Jealous, Kitty-Mingus, our silver Persian, fell on
her back, purring for a tummy rub. "Aww, don't you
widdle kitties worry; we'll be otay.

"Suppose your daddy hadn't built this place? We'd
be in trouble—probably in the air, spinning around
like the inside of a washing machine. Hey, you got any
food in here?"

"Oh, Sue Jan, you know we didn't have any time
to grab some food on our way down."

I wished we had. There was some leftover chicken-
fried steak and butter beans in the fridge and some
popovers from the night before. My stomach growled
at the thought.

She pointed to a shelf. "Well, what's that stuff over
there, then?"

"It's rations, you know, fallout shelter rations, the
kind that last for decades."

Sue Jan hopped up off the cot she'd been sitting on. She blew dust off a can. "Hey, this looks like peaches in syrup. I love peaches."

"Now wait a minute, Sue Jan. Those are special rations for. . .just in case anything were to happen." I grabbed at the can.

"Well, I have news for you." She tugged back. "Something *is* happening out there, and I'm not gonna die hungry when I have this can of dee-lishus peaches right here in my hands." She found a box of plastic spoons, plucked one out, and plopped down on a cot, arms clutching the can.

"Oh, all right, then." I gave up, too tired to fight.

"Where's your atomic can opener, Lovita?" She winked.

I smirked back and reached for one on a shelf above the cot opposite hers.

"Ugh!" The can opener slipped from my hands and fell to the floor, out of sight. A sigh escaped as I creaked down on bended knees to look for it.

Sue Jan made a few motions like she was going to help, but there's no way she was going to let go of that can of peaches.

A glimpse of something shiny under the cot caught my attention. "Aha, got it." Reaching blindly, I skimmed through a hutch or two of dust bunnies before my fingers wrapped around something small.

"My old decoder ring!" I sat back on the floor in disbelief.

"What?"

"You remember, Suey. We used to send secret

messages back and forth about cute boys and stuff. I lost it when I was ten. Never thought I would see this thing again. I just can't believe I found it after all these years."

"That's nice, Ita, but where's that can opener? Did you find that thing yet?"

Annoyed, I shimmied forward a bit to look and spotted it by the leg of the cot. "Here you go."

She snatched it from my hand, eager to get to the peaches.

I blew the dust off the ring and smiled. There were two wheels on it—alphabet and number. It was simple to work. Twenty-six letters of the alphabet. Turn the number code wheel one way and the corresponding letter was revealed. Of course, if you wanted a double or triple secret code, you assigned different numbers to letters. I tried to slide the ring on my index finger but it no longer fit. It did slip over my pinkie, though.

Curious, I flicked on a flashlight and knelt down for another look under the cot. A heap of something caught my eye. I grasped whatever it was and pulled it out. Papers. I blew a blanket of dust off.

"*Achoo!* Ita, what are you doing? Can't you see. . . *achoo*. . .I'm trying to eat?" Sue Jan liked those peaches so much that before she was finished with the first can, she had opened up a second.

"Sorry."

The papers turned out to be a bundle of letters bound by a faded blue satin ribbon. I pulled at the bow to undo it. The letter on top was addressed to my mother.

Boom! Ba-boom! I slipped them into my pocket

and jumped onto the cot next to Sue Jan.

"What's that?"

"I don't know, but I'm scared." Sue Jan dropped her plastic spoon.

"Me, too."

We hugged each other like when we were kids.

Boom-boom-boom!

I tilted my head to the side so I could hear better. "That sounds like somebody knocking. I could just swear it sounds like somebody knocking."

Boom-boom! The sound echoed through the door like thunder.

On instinct, I released the air lock and hissed open the door. Monroe tumbled in, a heavy stew pot in his hand. The wind blew in leaves with him, and I closed the door just in time enough to see my back screen door rip off and go flying.

"Monroe! What are you doing here?" Sue Jan stood up.

He bent over, sucking in air hard. His suit was all crumpled and twisted, and he smelled like a wet dog. I noticed that his eyes lit up when he raised his face and saw her. "Sue Jan, Lovita, I—I was driving home and I saw a big black tornado way past Pierson's farm across the way from your house. And I saw your car. So. . ." He paused to catch his breath again. "I ran in to warn you and couldn't find you. I followed the trail of mud to your pantry. You—your shelf was open. I started banging on this door with a pan, and here I am." He paused to suck in air. "What kind of room is this anyway?"

In our hurry, we must have left the secret shelf door open. "You mean you risked your life just to warn us?"

I asked, impressed.

His face flushed. "Well, no, I wouldn't say that. I just needed to tell you, to warn you about the tor—"

Sue Jan shoveled another spoonful of peaches in her mouth. "Ithz a fallouth sthelter." She swallowed. "You want some peaches, Monroe? These are some of the best peaches I ever did have."

Without hesitation Monroe answered. "Yes, Sue Jan, I do believe I would like some." He melted onto the cot next to her. "What kind of room did you say this was?"

"A fallout shelter." She held the can, gave him a spoon, and put the can in his lap, but I don't think I saw him take but two bites.

Twenty minutes later, it was starting to get a bit warm and claustrophobic inside, smelly, too, with Monroe in wet seersucker, not to mention the four kitties. I decided it was time to face the damage, whatever damage there was, behind the door. "Sue Jan, Monroe, I'm gonna open that door now. You ready?" I started to turn the wheel then stopped and leaned my head into the cold metal. "Please, Jesus, don't let my house be destroyed."

"Well this is a fine time to start praying, Lovita," snorted Sue Jan. "You should've been doing that *before* your house was all smashed up. Go on, Lovita. Open it."

I paused to sneer her way, drew in a breath, and finished turning the wheel. The air lock hissed and I swung it open.

"I'm going out with you, Lovita," said Monroe with determined bravado.

"We both are," added Sue Jan.

They shadowed me through the threshold and into the kitchen. "Hey," I was amazed to announce, "looks like everything's okay—so far." The kitchen floor was strewn with leaves that had blown in through the doorway, the screen door having been plucked right off its hinges. I found it in the front yard. The car was coated in muddy rain, leaves, and who knows what else, but it started up fine.

"I'm hungry." Sue Jan frowned as she flicked the light switch. "Electricity's out. Good thing this is a gas stove. Let's see what we have to eat." Sue Jan rummaged through the cupboard. She shouted with glee, "Funnel cake mix! I'm gonna make us some funnel cakes and good strong coffee."

"Okay, you do that, but then we've got to drive back into town and check up on everybody. I hope no one was hurt."

"Me, too," added Monroe. "That tornado was the scariest thing I ever did see. I hope I never see another one for the rest of my life."

"Well, I guess I'll go and sweep all these leaves out of my house." I laughed. "Maybe I should use my leaf blower."

Sue Jan tittered. "Hear that, kitties? Auntie Ita's being silly."

Monroe sneezed. "Sorry, I–I'm allergic to cats. If it's okay with you and Sue Jan, I'm going to go outside to hose off the cars and clear out some of the branches in your yard."

I smiled. "That's fine with me, Monroe. Thanks."

Sue Jan held up a spatula. "Did he just say he's

allergic to cats?" She turned her attention back to the stove. But not without a loud "hmmrph."

The smell of funnel cakes frying on the old gas stove soon drew us to the table. That and the smell of freshly brewed coffee. Kitty-Mingus, Hotdog, Vickie-Lou, and Sunshine sang a chorus of purrs over the mountains of food Sue Jan dumped in their bowls. Our plates were sprinkled with powered sugar over tasty swirls of fried dough and spooned mounds of sliced strawberries. The coffee was as good as it smelled. Monroe seemed overwhelmed with bliss.

"Thank you, Sue Jan." He wiped his mouth carefully, then he sneezed. "That was—that was—*achoo*—wonderful. I can't remember ever enjoying funnel cakes so much."

I burst out laughing.

"What's so funny, Ita? Monroe's sneezing tickle your funny bone?"

"I just thought of something." I laughed so hard I started snorting.

Sue Jan grabbed my arm, still oblivious to the joke. "Tell us."

"F–f–funnel cakes."

"What's so funny about—"

"Funnel clouds. Funnel cakes."

The three of us busted out laughing. Every time we thought we'd stop, the laughter started up again.

"Ita." Between howls, Sue Jan was trying to say something. "Ita, if I don't s–stop laughing I'm gonna piddle."

PEACH PIE ON THE SLY

It was impossible to drive down the town's main street without dodging some kind of debris. There were uprooted plants, branches, and leaves, trash from overturned cans, broken glass, and splintered wood everywhere. We dropped Monroe off by the filling station when he saw that a group of men needed some help with a massive oak branch blocking a side street. We parked our car as close to the shop as we could, which turned out to be a couple of blocks away.

The power company was already surveying the damage. A downed line in front of Callie's Texas Star Café left the entire block without electricity. I noticed Callie first; the familiar sprigs of honey-colored hair, usually pulled real neat away from her face, today hung in ringlets, styled by the wind. She waved to us and smiled from the shards of a big picture window when she saw us.

"Sue Jan, Lovita!" she called. "Why don't you girls come on in the café for a minute, huh? I'm not open for business yet, but you girls can set yourselves down and have a glass of milk with some peach pie I made earlier today."

We jumped over the power line and were through the door before the technician could open his mouth.

His eyes were sure open wide, though. I'm not sure whether he was shocked, scared, or mad over what we did. But Callie had said, "peach pie," and we answered the call.

For all the good food available in the café—big juicy burgers and hand-cut steak fries, chicken-fried steak with white gravy and real mashed potatoes, roasted chicken with braised carrots and corn on the cob—Callie Calloway was as thin as a telephone pole. Even though she passed the forty mark two years ago, her skin was smooth, clear, and without a wrinkle in sight. Her eyes were her best feature, though—a watery blue with little gold flecks, the most different-looking kind of eyes I have ever seen. Like eyes on a model or somebody famous. And Callie was nice, real nice. Everyone in town liked her, although Sue Jan used to be snippy to her for a time. There was a rumor that some guy Sue Jan had her eye on had taken Callie out on a date. Sue Jan got over it, though. There was no hating someone like Callie. She's just too nice a person.

The Texas Star Café had been around for a long time, since before I was born, though it used to be called Dodie's Lunch Bucket. When Miz Dodie passed on and none of her kids wanted to work the diner, they sold it to Callie. She got it at a good price, too, because it had been up for sale a couple of years, at least.

What I liked about the place was the smooth, fiftyish look of it. All the booths were gold Naugahyde, framed in polished chrome. And there was a music wheel at every table to select songs from. I usually fight Sue Jan for control of the wheel because she hogs it, playing all her favorites—"Purple People Eater," "Love Letters in the Sand," and "Yellow Rose of Texas."

Of course, eating at the lunch counter was fun, too, with the stools that swiveled and all, but not so comfortable for plus-size women like us. I once tried to sit on one and slid right off like an avalanche. Had a big bruise to show for it, as well as a newfound fear of falling. So I never sat on another stool. Maybe someday, when I lose weight.

We sat in the booth. Callie brought a tray with two big glasses of milk and wedges of fragrant peach pie.

"Ooh," Sue Jan squealed in delight at the first bite. Motioning with her fork, she said between chomps, "Callie, this is your best peach pie yet. . . . I mean it. . . . I really do."

"Well, I'm glad you like it." She smiled. "So how'd you girls fare in the tornado?"

"We're okay, Callie. My house took a little bit of a beating—some shingles missing and such, lots of branches and wood that'll need to go through the chipper. My screen door was blown clean off. But other than that, we fared well," I explained. "How about you?"

"I guess, all in all, the café's okay. Getting the electricity on is my main concern."

I took the opportunity to savor my first bite of the flaky, delicate crust and the sweet, peachy filling flavored with brown sugar and cinnamon. Callie must have seen the look of ecstasy on my face because she let me have a few more bites before she resumed talking.

"I used fresh peaches from Miller's farm. Old Man Miller made me a good deal on some crates at the farmer's market, and I couldn't resist. They were ripe and perfect. The smell of 'em is like perfume. Good, huh?"

I gave out a muffled "pherfect" between chews.

Sue Jan was already finished and licking the prongs of the fork. She scraped up every last atom of peach pie from the plate. If we were home she would surely have licked the dish, but since we were out in public, she maintained a sense of *day-corum*. Which surprised me.

A serious expression washed over Callie's face. "Girls, I didn't just ask you here to enjoy some milk and peach pie. I have another reason." She held a napkin in her fingers and kept twisting it into points then untwisting it. "I wondered—I mean, there's something I need to ask you."

Sue Jan pointed at her plate and interrupted. "Before you ask what you're gonna ask, do you mind if I have another piece of pie? I'll answer anything you want for another piece of pie. I'll give you all my account numbers, my driver's license, social security number, and probably all my money, if you ask me for it."

She shook her head, eyes twinkling. "My pie's that good, Sue Jan? Sure, go on ahead and cut yourself another piece from the pie case on the counter."

Before Callie finished her sentence, Sue Jan was halfway out of the booth. I don't think I've ever seen her move so fast. How she could even look at another peach was beyond me. She and Monroe had polished off two large cans of bomb shelter peaches—and I mean large.

I smiled and leaned forward. "Well, go on, Callie, shoot."

She blinked a few times and pursed her lips, wording her thoughts with care. "Do you think there's something strange going on around this town?"

I tilted my head, puzzled—then realized how stupid I must have looked doing that, like a golden retriever. "I don't know, Callie. Hmm, what kind of strange things are *you* talking about? 'Cause I had something unusual happen to me over lunch yesterday. There was a strange message in my fortune cookie, saying my daddy. . ." I choked on the undigested emotions. "Said my daddy was murdered and a man in a Stetson was gonna tell me something about it."

Her eyes widened. "You mean somebody killed your father?"

I stared back at her. Hearing her say it that way suddenly made me grasp the full impact.

"Y–yes."

She sat back, eliciting squeaks from the Naugahyde cushion. "Did you find out who sent you that message? Do you have any idea who might have done it or how?"

"No to all of your questions," I said. "But I wish I did."

Callie reached into her apron pocket, pulled out a business card, and handed it to me. She shook her curls. "Lots of folks come through this diner on their way to other places. I know my food's good, but not many people besides locals or folks from Bentley come here specifically."

I nodded in agreement. "That's true. Wachita's a small town." The card belonged to someone named John Smith, Geological Services Director, Claddoch Oil.

"Lately though, I've noticed a lot of new faces." She slowly twisted a fresh paper napkin. "At first I thought they were just coming through on their way to Bentley or some other place, but these same people show up every day for breakfast or lunch, sometimes for dinner. Which meant that they were staying somewhere nearby. When I bought the peaches from Old Man Miller, I saw 'em. Old Man Miller told me he was letting 'em rent a spot on his land for their trailers—had a three-month contract. But for the life of me, I can't figure out why."

I glanced around the café. *Where is Sue Jan?* "Excuse me for a second, Callie." I turned to look around the diner and called for Sue Jan. No answer.

How long could it take to dish up a slice of pie?

"She must've gone to the bathroom," Callie said.

I shrugged my shoulders. "Maybe. What's up with the business card? It says the man's a geologist. Maybe they're all rock hounds." I handed it back to her.

"This man was with a group of five men who claimed they were all geologists from an oil company based in Houston. For a tip, the man gave me his card with a twenty-dollar bill wrapped around it. Made a point of saying he'd appreciate hearing about any strange goings-on around town."

"Why would a geologist want to know about strange goings-on?"

"He said they were putting together a big deal and

some competitors were trying to move in on them."

Callie leaned forward and spoke in hushed tones. "These were men in expensive casual clothes and dark glasses."

"Were any of the men wearing cowboy hats?"

She seemed to think a minute. "No. They weren't the type."

After a sip of ice water, I had to say what was on my mind. "Callie, what's so strange about a bunch of geologists here in town? I mean, they're probably chipping away at rocks and such with their special hammers and all. What's the big deal?"

She shifted position in the smooth Naugahyde and threw down the napkin. "For most people, there wouldn't be anything strange about that. But you see, before I opened my café here in Wachita, I worked as a waitress in another town in Texas. An oil town. I've seen plenty of geologists. Got to know quite a few, and they all have something in common. They dress like slobs. Most of 'em, anyway. They don't go for the fancy, expensive clothes when they're out in the field."

"Really?" I asked, interested.

"Sure. They wear tie-dye shirts and old shorts with lots of pockets, T-shirts they've owned since college, with band logos nobody's ever heard of, and good hiking boots."

Sue Jan burst back into the room. "Whew, did you miss me, girls?"

"Where were you?" I asked, a touch of aggravation in my voice.

She giggled. "In the bathroom, of course, silly.

Besides, Ita, that's rude to ask. Anyway." She slapped the table and started talking fast. "It's about time for us to move on, Callie. It sure has been nice visiting with you, and the pie was fabulous. But Ita and I have got to get going to take a look at the shop. We might have to cover the roof with a tarp or something and call FEMA or the National Guard. So, let's go, Ita." She grabbed my arm and almost plucked me out of the booth.

I've known Sue Jan long enough to know there's something wrong when she wants to get away from a source of food. And it was obvious that she wanted to get out of the café real fast.

"Thanks, Callie. Sue Jan's right, we need to get going, but I'd like to come back tomorrow and talk about this some more if you have the time."

"Sure." She nodded. "Or you could call me. You have my number, don't you?"

"I have it somewhere, but just in case I have trouble finding it, would you mind jotting it down for me again?"

Callie walked to the counter to grab a paper napkin and pulled out a pen from her apron. That's when I heard the bell ring on the door. Sue Jan was already outside.

Somehow, the napkin slipped through my fingers to the floor. I bent down to retrieve it. *Why do I keep dropping things?* "Talk to you later, Callie."

"Okay, Lovita. Take it easy and please"—she raised her index finger to her lips—"keep this to yourself for now. Okay?" She looked both ways for emphasis.

A cold chill ran through me. "Should I be afraid?"

Her shoulders hunched up and down. "I don't know, Lovita. But just to be safe, let's be discreet. Okay?"

"Okay, bye." I opened the door and happened to look up on the way out. I noticed Callie's reflection in the big round shoplifting mirror above. She was holding up an empty pie tin and looking kind of confused.

That Sue Jan.

FENG SWAY

The sign Mama made for me was splintered into at least a dozen pieces. LOVITA'S CUT 'N STRUT, gone. My knees felt all wobbly. "I—I think I'm gonna b–be sick."

Sue Jan caught me before I sank to the ground. "Oh, Ita, I'm sorry." She stroked my head. "It's gonna be okay. We'll just have another sign made. I know it won't be the same, but the paint was starting to wear thin on this one anyway and. . ."

I flicked her hand off like I would a housefly. "Sue Jan, I can't believe that you would say that. In fact"—I pointed an accusatory finger at her—"I'll bet you're glad. You've been wanting me to get a new sign ever since it went up."

She looked me square in the eye. "Now, Lovita, you know that in time you would have had to get rid of that ratty ole sign anyway. You just couldn't bring yourself to do it."

"It's sentimental to me. You know that. My mama—"

"Your mama, Bessie Mae Horton, gave it to you at the grand reopening of the shop when she turned it over to you, Lovita. I know the story. I lived it with you. I was there, woman."

"Then you, of all people, know just how much

this old sign means to me, especially now. My daddy might have been murdered. Did you hear what I just said?" I brushed a tear away.

She took a step closer and made a motion as if to touch my arm again, but she didn't. "But you were there when he died, Ita."

"I know, but well, maybe he didn't die of a heart attack like we all thought. Or maybe he did, but it wasn't of natural causes."

We both stared down at the waterlogged shards of wood. Sue Jan reached down and picked up one of the sharp wood splinters. "Here, you want a toothpick? I still got some funnel cake stuck up in my teeth. I think it's that back tooth that always catches things."

I knocked the splinter of wood out of her hand. "You probably have a whole peach pie stuck in your teeth as well! I saw that empty pie tin. Did you take it into the storeroom and inhale it?"

Flustered in the face, Sue Jan stumbled back a feeble defense. "What are y—how could you even? I mean, why would I?"

"I know you did it because number one, I know you love peach pie. Number two, you disappeared for a half an hour and"—I held out my hands, palms up—"number three, I saw the empty pie tin in Callie's hands when I was leaving."

She threw her arms up, exasperated. "Oh all right. I ate the pie, but it was so yummy, I just couldn't get enough of it. I would have stayed up nights just thinking about those peaches in that flaky crust and—"

"Oh, why don't you just shut up, Sue Jan! You're

so selfish and besides that, you think you can quick fix everything in life with a joke. Some things are serious."

Sue Jan's mouth moved, but no words came out. Finally, she managed to spit out a few volleys. "I didn't mean to, I mean. . . Ita, of course I take it seriously."

In a low, purposeful voice, I released some angry thoughts brewing. "Y–you just never know when to keep your th–thoughts out of your mouth. Some ideas are better left in your head where they b–b–belong, and you know why? Because th–that's how you h–hurt people." On a roll, I kept going. Stopping was out of the question. I shook my index finger her way. "Y–you know y–you do, S–Sue Jan."

I turned my back to her and looked down the main street, littered with branches and bits of debris. Some people a block down were already hammering and sawing. I could smell the fresh-cut sawdust.

Sue Jan walked toward me, crunching over glass. Reluctant, I turned to face her.

"You know, Lovita, you might just be right." Smoothing her hair gently, she pursed her lips as if in deep thought. "I guess I am over the top. I like to joke around and, to be fair, you do, too. In fact, I know a lot of things about you. For instance, just now you started stuttering. I've been around you a long time and I just happen to know that you stutter when you get mad. The first time I noticed it was back in high school when you got mad at that boy who dumped you."

My eyes burned indignantly. "Rusty d–did not dump me."

She stepped up toe-to-toe. "Did, too."

"Did not." I scowled back.

"Rusty left you at the prom. Just took off right in the middle of it. He left you."

We stared each other in the eye. "Since you feel like talking about rejection, why don't we reminisce about some of *your* finer moments, Sue Jan?"

Sue Jan covered her ears and started singing real loud, " 'There's a yellow rose of Texas that I am going to see. . . .' "

"Bill Crass or Moss Harvey?"

" 'Nobody else could miss her, not half as much as me. . . .' "

"You remember them, don't you Sue Jan? If we're gonna talk about rejection, we need to have some fair play in this game."

" 'She cried so when I left her, it like to broke my heart. . . .' " She pressed her hands tightly against her head and looked to be concentrating real hard, like she was fixin' to shoot a basketball. " 'And if I ever find her, we nevermore will part.' "

I grasped her wrists and pulled them off her head. "Sue Jan, that's enough. Let's stop this."

She sighed in relief.

I rubbed my eye. "Sue Jan, I don't want to fight. I'm just too tired today."

"We've been through a lot today, with twisters and cleaning up after 'em and then seeing the shop all destructed."

"Destroyed," I corrected.

"Whatever."

Loud rattling and squeaking noises interrupted our conversation, followed by yelling.

"Oh no, Ita, it's Hazel and Inez." Sue Jan hid behind me.

I turned round and round, but she stuck behind me closer than a shadow at noonday. "Sue Jan, if you are entertaining the notion that you can hide yourself behind me, then I need to ask you a couple of questions; just *how* fat do you think I am? And how much skinnier do you think *you* are?"

"Shh," she whispered, "they might hear."

I grasped her arm and pulled her out in front to face me. "No, you shush, Sue Jan. What are you afraid of?"

She grasped my shoulders. "They're always trying to get me to the altar."

"Married?" I quipped. "Oh that, you know they always say that to me, too."

"No, Lovita," she interrupted. "Saved. They're always trying to git me in church."

Hazel Murray and Inez Nunez belong to my church, and they were my mama's best friends. Everyone in town agreed that they had been an interesting trio when Mama'd been alive. Bessie Mae, of Irish descent, had been a fair-skinned, freckle-faced, brown-haired beauty, whereas Hazel, black, big-boned, and beautiful, used to turn heads with her high cheekbones, full lips, and fancy hairstyles. As for Inez, her glossy licorice black hair, creamy café au lait skin, and large brown eyes were so striking, strangers used to ask if she was a Latin movie star. Inez didn't used to be big like Mama and Hazel, but she sure was now. One thing all three had in common was a sizable love for Jesus and a not-so-subtle way of sharing that love everywhere they went. Hazel and Inez carried on that tradition after Mama passed.

"Lovita Mae Horton and Sue Jan Pritchard!" Hazel yelled. "Purr-raise the Lord, you're all right!" She paused. "You girls are all right, aren't you?" Hazel was the only woman I knew who could send her voice way ahead of her body, like a Dolby speaker. She was still half a block away, hat flapping up and down, rattling toward us with a silver grocery cart piled high. "Purr-raise Jesus." We could hear what she had to say as if she were standing right next to us.

Hazel and Inez headed up the town's Barbecue Crew, a team of volunteers who took care of business whenever the townsfolk had need. Sometimes they got together to raise money to pay a hospital bill or rebuild somebody's house after a fire took it. Any kind of bad news, or in this case, bad storm, would summon up the Barbecue Crew. A parade of people would soon follow, with baskets of fresh-baked biscuits, pies, cobblers, and brownies. The men would set up tables and fill smokers with trays of beef, pork, and deer sausage. My mouth was already watering just thinking about all that good food.

"*Hola, chiquitas.*" Inez waved. Her shopping cart wobbled off course under one-handed direction and smashed into a water-saturated crape myrtle on the sidewalk. A cluster of pink blossoms showered Inez's hair. The drops of water shimmered off her dyed-black-as-a-seal's-back bouffant, like rhinestones.

"Hi, Miz Hazel—Miz Inez. How're you two doing?" I asked, smiling and waving.

Hazel's voice vibrated through the air. "Inez, watch where you're going. Now you're all soggy. You're makin' your guardian angel work overtime." A whoosh of wind blew round the corner, as if in heavenly reply, and shook raindrops off a cluster of green leaves onto Hazel's pink hat, sparing her peppery gray hair underneath.

Sue Jan and I shared muffled giggles. Leaning hard on her shoulder, I tried like mad to get control of myself. "Suey, I haven't been called a chiquita since I *was* a chiquita."

"I know," she snickered back. "Here we are, thirty-six-year-old women, and they still think of us as little girls."

As if they were NASCAR drivers, the older women swerved their shopping carts past all the debris and, after stopping just short of us, they pounced on us with hugs, kisses, and exclamations. Hazel looked younger than her sixty-five years and was definitely stronger than anyone would imagine. She somehow managed to enclose both of us in a bear hug and, as soon as she let go, Inez pinched our cheeks till they hurt. The only volume control on Inez was loud and louder. As she talked, I couldn't help but notice that the powder pink frosted lipstick she wore extended over the natural edges of her lips into a heart shape. Though it contrasted well with her skin, the frosting didn't work. It was too young for her. Sue Jan caught my look, and her eyes widened till I could see the whites all around. Without letting go of our cheeks, Inez opened her mouth to speak. "My babies, all grown up into beautiful women now. . .but why, *por que*, you not married yet? Huh?"

"Uh-hmm, that's the same question on my mind," Hazel added, arms folded like she meant business.

"Well, ah." I coughed, fidgeting with the straps on my purse. I tried to change the subject. "Hey, what are the carts full of food for?"

Eyes set in solid contact, Inez continued without missing a beat. "The street's all blocked up. We park three blocks away." She held up three fingers for emphasis. "And had to haul our food. So we find these baskets. The churches are join together to have a big barbecue in the middle of town because no one has 'lectricity, and *why* you not married?"

Sue Jan jumped in to the rescue. Striding confidently toward the crape myrtle tree, she leaned on one of its branches. "Now ladies, you know as well as we do how hard it is to find a good man around here. There's only a handful of respectable marriage-minded men in Wachita and Bentley combined."

"You shoulda' say so earlier." Inez leaped forward, obviously eager to comment. Straightening her floral duster, she said, "We'll be happy to find you girls some husbands." She took off her glasses, folded them, and pointed our way. "Maybe you two. . .too picky. We'll find you some good husbands."

"That's our mission in life," Hazel added matter-of-factly, straightening her glasses. Before you could sneeze, she bounced into prayer. "Lord Jesus, these two fine maidens need some bridegrooms of their own. And, Lord Jesus, we ask that You scour the earth or this blessed town of Wachita to find them the soul mates that You have chosen for them. Righteous, upstanding men, who have jobs. Looks don't matter according to 2 Corinthians 4:16, 'though our outward man is perishing, yet the inward man is being renewed day by day.' No, Lord Jesus, only the man inside is what matters—"

"Excuse me."

"What?" Hazel's eyes flew open. She always kept them closed when she prayed, and it was obvious she wasn't used to being interrupted.

Sue Jan cleared her throat and stepped forward real tentatively. "Miz Hazel, about the prayer. You know the part where you prayed that looks don't matter and all? Well, would you mind praying instead like it does matter? I mean, if you're gonna pray and all." She laughed. "Not like praying makes any difference. But I could use all the help I can get."

"What she say?" asked Inez as if she hadn't really heard.

Though in silent agreement with Sue Jan about the looks department, I elbowed her. "Oh no, you shouldn't have."

Hazel looked up at the sky. White clouds reflected off her large bifocals. "Father God, hold on a minute while I put the fear of the Lord in this here girl."

Sue Jan's face turned white as a sheet. She reached out to Hazel to pat her shoulder, now hard as a stone. "T–that's okay, Miz Hazel, and"—she turned to Inez—"and Miz Inez. Forget I said anything. I—I don't know what I was thinking. Really." She turned to me, wringing her hands, and begged, "Tell them, Lovita."

Inez was already immersed in prayer, hands raised.

Before I could open my mouth, Hazel's index finger raised slowly and straightened above her head, like the staff of Moses preparing for battle, or to part the Red Sea.

Sue Jan panicked and she began babbling. "I—I changed my mind. That's right, I changed it. Doesn't matter to me what a"—Sue Jan tittered—"man, or I mean, husband looks like. Ugly's fine with me. He could look like his face caught on fire and somebody put it out with a chain, for all I care." She prattled on, " 'Cause you're right, looks—looks are just not important." She nodded her head like a bobble doll, hoping they would suddenly agree.

Hazel removed her pink floppy hat and placed it with care in the basket. The air seemed to crackle around us.

Sue Jan backed up in fear. Her heel caught in a piece of waterlogged wood, and she leaned over to pull it off. "You know what I said about prayer." Sue Jan laughed nervously. "I don't know why I said a thing like that. Of course I believe in the power of prayer. Why, who doesn't?" She looked around hoping to draw somebody's support.

Inez was still praying, but louder than before, leaning hard on the front of the shopping cart as if it were an altar. I couldn't quite make out what she was praying, because over half of it was Spanish mixed with English.

Miz Hazel spoke without looking at any of us, like she was talking to that still small voice in her head. "You know what they say about drawing an unbeliever with cords of love, Lord Jesus, and if You can't draw 'em with cords of love, You can hit 'em with a cord of wood."

"Amen," praised Inez.

Sue Jan looked at the piece of wood in her hand, then she looked up at Miz Hazel and threw it down like it was on fire.

Hazel laughed. "Sue Jan, what do you think? I'm not going to spank you. You're not a little girl anymore. But I am going to ask you for a promise." She embraced Sue Jan's cheeks in her palms. "Just promise me, baby, that you'll come to church this Sunday." Hazel's face reflected tender love and patience. "You need to check out the gospel and decide for yourself whether you believe."

Sue Jan's eyes shifted back to me. I nodded in support, and her expression relaxed. "Well, I guess I could. I do need some special prayers about this dinner I'm cooking."

But just then, as if it were planned, and there's no way it could have been, a crowd of church ladies and townsfolk arrived. Camera crews from channels 7 and 9 had showed up, as well, to cover the damage and devastation, even though there wasn't much in the way of devastation to cover. The rest of the Wachita Barbecue Crew followed and unwittingly saved Sue Jan from the gospel truth. But not for long.

7

SWEET, SOUR, AND SAUCY

Squeezed into a lawn chair in the middle of Main Street, Sue Jan sighed with contentment in the dusty glow of early evening and tapped Monroe on the arm. He had joined the Barbeque Crew to help set up the pits, chairs, and tables but was still wearing his soggy seersucker suit. Good thing it was pretty much wash and wear.

She patted her stomach. "I'm as full as a tick. I never dreamed I could eat so much food—and still be hungry, but I could go for just a little something later at Cheng's place. The smell of that yummy Chinese food is driving me crazy. Some hot and sour soup, egg rolls, fried rice, and wontons, maybe a small order of sweet-and-sour pork. Or," she added, "we could split one."

"Sure, Sue Jan," the doting Monroe replied. "Whatever you want."

I shook my head in disbelief and looked her square in the eye. "Sue Jan, this is like déjà vu. You know you never split anything. The only thing you like to split is the meal ticket. You wind up eating ninety-five percent of the food, and I still pay for half. No thank you."

Almost all the folks in town had rolled up their sleeves to clean up the streets and either contribute to or prepare the meal, smack dab in the middle of town.

Lovita's Cut 'n Strut needed a new window and sign. The inside took a beating from the rain, too. With the Sheetrock soggy and all the blow-dryers, curling irons, and flatirons, too, the beauty shop was pretty much a mess. However, the boutique part of the shop was fine since there was no window nearby. Plus, half the new stock wasn't put out yet because the storm interrupted that. But the shop would for sure not reopen until some serious remodeling took place. And that meant big bucks. Insurance would cover only so much. The kind I had covered the bare minimum, like a broken umbrella in a rainstorm.

Hazel and Inez were still busy serving up seconds and thirds to people, but every now and then I could see them looking our way and other women glancing over from hushed whispers. The word had gone out to all the intercessors in town, and Sue Jan seemed the object of many a fervent prayer. *Look out, Sue Jan.* I smiled to myself and silently added my own small prayer on her behalf.

After gorging ourselves on plates piled high with Texas barbequed brisket and sausage, pinto beans slow cooked in bacon and cilantro, potato salad, and jalapeño corn bread, we sat immobile in lawn chairs in the waning light of a perfect evening, with over half the town.

Old Man Miller and Callie walked by, deep in conversation. Callie shot me a glance out of the corner of her eye, and then in a louder-than-normal voice, she asked, "So the storm blew one of those trailers over, huh? It's a miracle no one was hurt."

That Callie was sure on the ball.

I felt something poking my thigh and realized that the bundle of letters I'd found in the shelter under my house was still in my skirt pocket. The decoder ring was still on my finger, too. Eager to have a look at the letters, I pulled them out and opened the one on top first. The paper, dated about a month before Daddy died, was creased and yellowed, the ink faded. I could still read the neat handwriting. I recognized it right away as Daddy's.

> *Dearest B,*
> *How can I convince you that there is no one else*
> *but you in my life and in my heart?*

The rest of the letters slid off my lap as I sat up straight and pulled the paper up closer. I continued reading, holding the first letter with my right hand while the left groped around to retrieve the other letters.

> *I know I've been traveling a lot lately,*
> *sweetheart, but it's part of an investigation. The*
> *matchbooks from all the Chinese restaurants are*
> *the places I ate. Thought I would save them for the*
> *fallout shelter. To tell the truth, I'm starting to think*
> *that kind of food doesn't agree with me anymore.*
> *My stomach's been complaining about it and*
> *sometimes I get a headache. I got a fortune in a*
> *cookie the other day that said, "Your perseverance*

will pay off." *Not that I believe in any of that
stuff, mind you. But perseverance and patience are
important in my job, that's for sure.*

*I'll be home before you know it. Kiss our
Ita for me, and I'll save one for you when I get
home. Wink. Wink.*

*Love,
Your Clark*

Sue Jan and Monroe were laughing with a group
of children chasing bubbles from half a dozen bubble
wands. Oblivious to the shock that I imagined was
surely plastered across my face.

The next letter was from Mama to Daddy in response.

Dear Clark,

*I am sorry about the scene I caused with
Hazel and Inez last week. I've had time to
think about things since you're out of town
again, and realize now that you and I should
have discussed this matter in private.*

*When I first walked into Cheng's, and Loo
was standing by your table, talking to you and
smiling, I felt that my suspicions were justified.
She's so beautiful and exotic looking. And you'd
spent so much time there the last couple months,
when you were in town. So I thought. . .well,
then you know what I thought, don't you?*

*Anyway, when Fritz came back to the
table, I knew that you were telling the truth
about having lunch with him. So please forgive*

me for ever doubting you.

> *Yet I still feel that you're being secretive
> about something, Clark. When you come back
> from New Mexico, let's talk and clear the air.*

> *Faithfully yours,*

> *B*

Unable to continue, I folded the letters and bound them with the tattered ribbon. I tucked the letters back into my pocket. *Mama suspected Daddy of having an affair? With Loo, of all people?* I tucked my thoughts away, determined to save them for the quiet of the night, in my own bed, in my own room. The tears were brimming in back of my eyes, waiting for the go-ahead. I squeezed my eyes shut for a moment. *Not now!*

When I opened them, I noticed that even Fella, Dr. Nasale's ancient yellow Lab, had made it to the center of town. He approached me and greeted me with a lick to my hand. Fella's sweet eyes, framed in gray lashes, looked tired. I stroked his face and patted his gray-haired back. "There's a Fella, yes, he's a good old dog, a Fella." His tail swooshed back and forth like a fan.

Dr. Nasale shuffled behind his canine companion.

"Doc, would you mind talking to me for just a minute?" I patted the lawn chair next to me.

"Sure, Lovita." He lowered himself with care into the aluminum frame of the chair, sighed, and met my eyes.

I took a deep breath. "I need to ask you something about my father."

He blinked once and offered a palsied nod.

"Was he. . . Do you remember if he had any health problems?"

Dr. Nasale brushed some dog hairs off his pants leg. "As I recollect. . .let's see. . .come to think of it, yes. Your father was having some heart palpitations and breathing difficulties for at least a month before he died. I wanted him to go to Houston and have some tests done, and he was going to." Doc reached out to pat my arm. "Most likely it was a heart attack he died from."

"So you're sure?"

He chomped his jaws together the way old people do, and I noticed a patch of gray whiskers on his cheek the razor had missed. "Not a hundred percent. Sure looked like it to me. He had all the symptoms. Your mother described them to me afterward. It was hard on her, you know."

I blinked. "Doc, I've got to ask you this. I hope you don't mind. Was my mother—in love—with my father?"

He seemed confused by the question. Then his watery eyes shimmered, and he smiled. "If your parents weren't in love, then they were the greatest actors since John Barrymore and Myrna Loy."

I smiled back and covered my mouth with my hand to hold in a little gasp of relief. Whoever those two people Dr. Nasale mentioned were, my guess is they were in love. *Guess I was wrong about the doc having a mind like a steel sieve.*

He stood up and straightened out by degrees, then

he turned to me, kind eyed and caring. "Now, Lovita, since your father died early of heart problems, you should really have a thorough checkup. Call me."

I reached over to squeeze his hand. "Thanks, Doc."

He smiled and shuffled off toward his family sitting in a cluster of chairs near the barbershop.

"Lovita," Sue Jan said, staring at Fella with a splash of disapproval. "Why are you petting that mangy old dog?"

I glared her way. "Mangy? He's not mangy." I looked back down at Fella. "Don't listen to that woman rant. It's not you. She's a cat person—hates dogs in general." As if offended, Fella licked my hand, then he padded off after his master.

"Do you really hate dogs, Sue Jan?" Monroe asked, surprised.

Her face flushed. Sue Jan, a passionate cat person, was militant about the cats-versus-dogs issue. "You bet I do."

"Oh, don't get her started, Monroe," I begged, then, trying to change the subject, I said, "I'm glad we were able to put that closed-for-renovation sign up in front of the shop, but I'm sad about it, too. The shop's a mess, and I don't know how long it's gonna take to fix it up."

Sue Jan sat forward in her lawn chair, which squeaked and groaned under her weight. "You know, Lovita, I've been meaning to talk to you about something for a long, long time."

"About what?" I questioned, curious.

She sucked in her cheeks, "Wellll, you know we've been friends forever and working together for years now. Lovita's Cut 'n Strut has been my place of employment since I got out of high school with you."

Now I was really interested. "What are you getting at, Sue Jan?"

She covered her face in her hands, and though the words were a bit muffled, I heard her loud and clear. "I want to be a full partner with you and own half of Lovita's Cut 'n Strut and change the name 'cause I think it's horrible." Then, her hands came down slowly, peekaboo style. Her face was calm—even relaxed now, as if just getting those words off her chest had set her free of some burden.

"No way." The words flew out of my mouth before I could think. "Mama gave *me* that shop, not *you*. Last time I checked *I* was an only child. And, Sue Jan, as much as I think of you as a sister, you're not."

Monroe hopped up to get out of the line of fire. "I'm, ah, going to go and get you ladies something to drink. Be right back." He disappeared past a cluster of lawn chairs.

Heads were starting to turn, so I lowered my voice to a frantic whisper. "How could you even ask that, Sue Jan? This one—this one really takes the cake. You've pulled a lot of things over the years, but—"

"I know I'm not your sister, Lovita. Nobody's sister and nobody's daughter. I'm an orphan. Remember? Who was raised by a mean, hateful aunt who made my life miserable growing up. Being friends with you was the only bright spot in my life. But that has nothing whatsoever to do with what I'm talking to you about right now. We're talking about making a business decision, not about our friendship or inheriting something."

If I had a rewind or a do-over button, I would have used it to take back what I said. My heart broke for her. "I—I'm sorry, Sue Jan. I didn't mean to say what I said."

Hands at her temples, she closed her eyes, held them shut a moment, and then reopened them. "I was afraid this was how you would react, Lovita. Your whole identity is tied up in being the owner of Lovita's Cut 'n Strut, and the reality is that you're scraping to make ends meet."

"I—I—what do you mean? How could you say that?"

Sue Jan popped a mint into her mouth and offered the box to me. "Because it's true, that's why. I know how much you bring in and what your overhead is. And you're way over your head."

I turned my face away. "I don't want to talk about this right now, and I cannot believe you brought this up."

Sue Jan clucked on the mint in her mouth with serious intent. "*Now* is just the time to talk about it, Lovita. *Now* that the shop is all smashed up and all. *Now* that no money is coming in. *Now* that you have no customers."

Her eyes took on a dreamy quality. "I have ideas for the shop to modernize it. Maybe paint the walls glossy tomato red and add some beads and glittery cheetah print curtains at the stations or a disco ball for glamour. We could have giant high-heel chairs covered in crushed velvet or a zebra pattern for the customers in the waiting area. And I'd like to hang posters of hunky handsome movie stars on the ceiling above the wash stations so when people are gittin' their hair washed, they'd have something pleasant to look at. We could take on another stylist, too, and—"

Monroe returned with two plastic cups and held them up. "It's lemonade. They ran out of iced tea. Hope that's okay."

It was a perfect time to change the subject. Again. "Are you up for Cheng's, Monroe?" I asked.

"Well, sure," he answered. "I guess." He patted his midsection as if in pain. "I don't think I'll eat very much, though. I may have reached my limit."

From the corner of my eye, I noticed a couple of men I didn't know, strolling toward Cheng's, and remembered what Callie told me. Sure enough, they sported dress khakis, Izods, and dark sunglasses. One was a few inches taller than the other, though both had dark brown hair. They were dressed, and trying to look, casual. As if they fit in with the rest of Wachita. But they didn't.

I reached over to tap Monroe and Sue Jan, and I nodded toward the strangers.

Sue Jan narrowed her lids for a better look. "Nice change of subject, Ita, but we'll be talking about this again for sure. And, no, I don't know ' em. . .but they're cute." She rowed back and forth with her arms in an attempt to get up out of the lawn chair. "Let's go introduce ourselves."

I shrugged. "Sue Jan, looks like they're eating at

Cheng's and that's exactly where we're headed. We can make our acquaintance with 'em there." The metal chair squeaked and groaned as I lifted myself out of it. Two woven bands popped out. All because of my weight. I pinched my right arm to hold back the tears and hoped nobody noticed.

"Let's get going," I urged, without a trace of the emotions I felt inside. But Sue Jan had seen it all. Without having to say a word, she sent me a look of compassion with a slow blink of her eyes. How could someone be so wonderful and so aggravating at the same time?

8

PEKING DUCK AND COVER

The facade of Cheng's Dragon Inn was gold, red, and gaudy. Sue Jan loved it but I thought it looked scary. Two large ornamental tigers, spray painted gold, guarded the door. I shuddered as we passed the threshold and noticed the suffocating smells of candle wax and incense. The Lucky Buddha fountain to my right wasn't bubbling as usual and the cash register was out, too. Electricity hadn't been restored. Loo, "the Dragon Lady," as she liked to be called, was handwriting receipts and making change out of a red silk fanny pack around her waist.

As she approached us, a slight smile crackled her jaw. "Sue Jan, Lovita, and—who's this?" She tapped her temple in thought. "Monroe?" She bowed her head for a moment. "Welcome back to Wachita. I was told that you had returned, but had not the pleasure of crossing paths."

Monroe attempted an awkward return bow.

I saw Loo through different eyes now after reading the letters. *Was she. . .could she be. . .the other woman?* Loo's hair, dyed black, was always pulled back from her face in a severe knot. I've always had a secret theory about that. I think that the reason Loo always did her hair up that way was to give herself an instant face-lift. And if that was her goal, it was working out real good because her skin seemed pretty smooth for a woman in her sixties. She was thin, too. In her day, she might have been considered good-looking. But tonight she wore one of her usual silk dresses, red with a yellow frog fastener diagonal to her neck. Two red chopsticks, strung with hanging jade beads, pierced and crisscrossed the severe bun on her head. A smear of hastily applied red lipstick, some on her pearly whites, completed her fashion statement.

She had run Cheng's, with iron-handed efficiency, ever since her German husband, Fritz, died suddenly of a massive stroke. About the same time my daddy died.

Sue Jan was already tippy-toeing up and down like an elevator to look over Loo's head for a glimpse of the two men we had seen. The restaurant was sectioned off into private booths and clusters of two or three tables. Silk screens and walls of huge bamboo plants separated the different areas and gave patrons the illusion of a quiet, intimate dinner.

Loo led us to a table in the middle of the restaurant. "How's this?"

Sue Jan craned her neck and pushed past us. "Uh, no, Loo, that just won't do."

Monroe and I looked at each other and burst into laughter at the unintentional rhyme.

"What are you laughing at?" Sue Jan glared without really wanting an answer.

Then I caught something unusual. Loo shot a look at the waiter standing nearby. A look that spoke out an order without words. For some reason, Loo wasn't happy with us.

"How about right here?" Sue Jan pointed at a table

toward the back of the room. Loo nodded her head in acknowledgment. Just as she did, the waiter walked by with a bus tray and bumped into it, spilling the contents all over the table Sue Jan wanted. Every eye in the restaurant was on us, or trying to peek through the bamboo screens.

The waiter kept bowing and apologizing. Loo seemed angry at him, but her halfhearted scolding didn't ring true in my ears. It was enough, however, to send the man scrambling back to the kitchen.

"So sorry, Sue Jan, Lovita, and Monroe." She bowed then tried to lead us back to the original table. But Sue Jan wasn't having any of that. She folded her arms and tapped her foot.

"Loo, I want this one." Just then, the waiter popped back out of the kitchen with someone's order. The Dragon Lady shot him a look. He blinked a slow deliberate blink, handed the tray off to another waiter, and stepped forward to switch out tables for us. Sue Jan pushed past him as soon as the table touched the ground, and claimed it. A good strategy. In fact, Sue Jan could not have chosen a better one. It was right next to the two men who had by now removed their dark sunglasses to gawk at us in the candlelit interior.

"Right here is good, Loo." Sue Jan turned a charming smile toward the two men and mouthed a delicate *hi*. Of course, she made sure she was sitting back-to-back with one of them. I knew the trick. Pretty soon, Sue Jan would push her chair out instead of in, and slam into the back of the stranger's chair. That would be an icebreaker leading into an hour or two of nonstop flirtatiousness.

"Okay then, Monroe," she said, giggling, "as I recall, you agreed to split dinner with me. So let's order the lobster kew, shrimp fried rice—"

I made a sawing motion with my hands to interrupt. "While you two are ordering 'a little something,' I think I'll go to the ladies' room. If Loo comes while I'm gone, order me a large egg drop soup, cashew chicken, and the special everything fried rice." I know Sue Jan didn't hear, but Monroe gave me the thumbs up.

As I walked past the tables on the way to the ladies' room, I stopped to say hello to a bunch of different friends, neighbors, and customers. Seemed like people were more than willing for a candlelight dining experience tonight. Of course it probably wasn't easy for the chefs in the kitchen. Although they were cooking with gas, the electricity was still out. Kinda hard to see what you're cooking when it's dark inside.

A man in a dark booth tipped his head to me as I passed. *Do I know him?* His face, tanned and weathered like a crumpled grocery sack. I sort of smiled as if I recognized him, trying all the while to remember if I'd ever seen him before.

The ladies' room, empty save for an array of large candles across the washbasin, was deodorized with the overwhelming scent of Lysol masked with vanilla and carnation. The gold standard of gas station restroom fragrances. Three-dimensional dragon-themed wall-paper from the sixties or seventies still decorated the interior. The red, black, and gold colors were disturbing, yet familiar in an odd sort of way. The effect, achieved by black felt on the dragon's tail, had seen better days. There were places on the wall where people had touched it so many times the felt was actually worn away. I loved that wallpaper.

Loo was a stickler about certain things. One was that the bathroom soap had to be a Tiger Balm bar, specially formulated soap imported from China. The smell of it was pleasant enough, but I never could quite put my finger on what it reminded me of. I dried my hands on pull-down cloth towels, and then opened the squeaky, padded red door to exit.

To the right, farther down the dimly lit hallway to the kitchen, I noticed a bin filled with fortune cookies. *Forgive me, Lord. I have to find out.* I knew if I thought about it a moment more, I wouldn't do it, so I forced my legs to move fast. I stuffed a couple of handfuls in my purse and turned to make a hasty exit.

"Ma'am?" The man from the booth stood in the corridor, hat in his hands.

I swooned backward in surprise. *Caught.*

Heart pounding, I asked, "Yes?"

"I wonder if you could spare a few minutes of your time."

Though something about his face seemed kind enough and somehow familiar, I recalled my mama's warning about talking to strange men. "No, I don't think so. I don't know who you are and I'm here with friends, two friends who. . ." The last words came out in a rush, "Who are wondering where I am right now."

He opened his coat. I was about to scream and scramble past him, when I saw a glint of silver—a Texas Ranger star.

I gulped back my initial fear. "What can I do for you?"

"Ma'am, or should I say, Miz Lovita M. Horton, would you do me the honor of sitting in my booth for a few minutes and answering some questions?"

"How did you know my name? I—I guess so but I can't stay long. Well, I'll try my best to answer any questions you have. I don't know what they are, but whatever they are, I'll try."

I followed him slowly to the booth, casting glances to my right and left in an effort to be noticed. If this man were some kind of fake or a Howdy Doody serial killer, I needed someone to notice me. But all the people who had stopped me on the way to the bathroom didn't even bother to look up from their food when I passed this time. And the food did smell good, awful good. I hoped Monroe remembered to place my order.

The ranger's table was set for two. Once I was sitting across from him, he handed me a plain white business card. Clint Greech. A cell phone number was the only other printing on the card.

Just then, the server came with a tray of steaming-hot dishes. To my surprise, he placed a large egg drop soup, cashew chicken, and the special everything fried rice in front of me, and a large bowl of soup in front of the man.

A look of earnestness on his face, he waved at my plate. "I hope you don't mind that I had your order sent here instead."

Preoccupied with his business card, I merely mouthed the name—Clint Greech. Where had I heard that name before? I looked up. "Your name sounds so familiar to me, Mr. Greech. Did you by any chance know my daddy, Clark W. Horton?"

"Yes, I did." He winked. "In fact, your father and I worked together. You're probably too young to remember this, but I said a few words at his funeral."

"Sixteen. That's how old I was." I pointed his way, excited. "I used to call you Mr. G.—you're Mr. G."

"Yes." He nodded. "But since you're all grown-up now, call me Clint."

He looked different. I remembered Mr. G as a tall, lanky man with smooth, tanned skin and a quiet way about him.

"I miss him."

He reached over and took my hands in his. "Me, too."

He broke the seriousness of the moment with a short laugh as he picked up his spoon. "Lovita, why don't we go ahead and start eating? Food's getting cold as we speak." He offered a blessing, spoon in hand, and then started digging right in. Guess he was mighty hungry.

I was thankful that he broke the mood, because a dam of emotions was about to break. Sometimes the sad feelings I get from losing my daddy so young in life just hit me that way. You never stop missing the people you love. And you never stop loving them.

Sue Jan always says that she and I were born with at least one leg hollow to put away all the food. Honestly, I don't know where I put all that Chinese food on top of the barbeque feast we had earlier, on top of the peach pie at Callie's, and the funnel cake and strawberries before that, and the biscuit-and-sausage breakfast I had before leaving for work.

We reminisced a bit more between bites, and then a serious look crossed his face. "Lovita, I have something to tell you."

Flustered by this sudden change in gears, a simple "What?" dropped out of my mouth. To tell the truth, though, that strange clammy feeling was coming over me again. I forced a long sip of tea.

Clint laid his spoon down and wiped his mouth with a napkin. "It's about your father."

The waiter appeared at just that moment to refill our tea glasses and leave the bill.

My head began to pound in pace with my heart. And a strange, dizzy feeling spiraled through me. I'd felt it several times before, but not as bad as this. I never mentioned it to anyone, though—just figured I was coming down with something. But I made a mental note to see Dr. Nasale about it. No harm in checking it out.

Clint pulled the bill toward him and gave me a look. "No protesting allowed. I'm picking up the tab."

I drew in a short breath when I noticed two fortune cookies on the little black tray. Perspiration beaded across my forehead.

"Are you okay?" A sudden look of concern spotlighted on me.

I nodded. The feeling was already beginning to pass. "I–I'm okay now, I guess. Maybe all the excitement today got to me."

Clint opened a buck leather wallet and dropped a bill on the tray. Then he pushed it to the side, picked up the cookies, and placed one in front of each of us.

I couldn't move, like one of those golden tiger statues.

He pulled an envelope out of his pocket. "My wife, Sandie, and I moved to Austin after your father died. Not long ago, I received a package in the mail, addressed to me with no return address, postmarked from Houston. A lone fortune cookie. And inside it was a message."

I looked from his face to the envelope and back to his face.

"Go on," he urged, nodding toward the envelope. "Open it."

The plain white paper had one simple message printed down the middle:

Clark was murdered. Meet me in Wachita on April 5th at 10:00 p.m. across the street from Lovita's Cut 'n Strut.

"Then that was you?" I pointed, mouth hinged open.

"Me?" he asked, confused, mid-sip into his iced tea.

"Yesterday. The man in the Stetson, outside my shop."

He reached down next to him and lifted the hat to show me. But still confused, he asked, "How did you know that?"

Digging through my purse like Sue Jan, I started pulling out curlers and change and about ten ink pens, my wallet, a complete makeup kit, some candy bars, two kinds of nail polish, a banana, and finally, the tiny slip of paper I was looking for—the fortune cookie fortune from yesterday's lunch.

Your father was murdered. A man in a Stetson will tell you more tomorrow.

The lids around his eyes squeezed close together. "Lovita, when and where did you get this?"

"Chun's, yesterday," I answered. "Sue Jan and I have lunch there every Thursday. It came in my fortune cookie at lunch."

Clint asked, "Do you have any idea who might have sent you this message?"

"No. I asked Tan if he knew anything about it, and he said no. He checked with the chef for us, too."

"I think I remember Tan from years back. Is he a waiter?"

I took a sip of tea. "Tan is the owner, and he waits on tables."

Intense green eyes stayed focused on mine. "Can I keep it?"

I looked back at him. "If you didn't send the note, how did whoever sent this know you would wear a Stetson? Are you gonna use this to try and find out who wrote it?"

"Yes, I'm taking this seriously. And in answer to your first question—I've always worn one." He reached over to drum on the brim. "It's sort of my signature look."

I knocked on the table and leaned back. "Then keep the fortune. To tell the truth, it gives me the creeps." I paused and looked away so I wouldn't cry.

"I'm going to investigate this matter thoroughly, Lovita, and I will share my findings with you at the appropriate time." He added with a forced smile of reassurance, "It's probably nothing, though. Just some prank."

I eyed the fortune cookie in front of me.

He noticed my hesitation. "Go ahead and open it," Clint urged.

Using the prong of my fork, I pierced the wrapper puffed with air, and then broke the cookie clean in half, which doesn't happen very often. The message in red ink seemed to jump out.

> *"The best things in life are free.*
> *Except this dinner."*

I read it out loud and looked at Clint. We burst out laughing.

He grinned. "Now that's more like it."

I held up my hand. "But technically not true since you paid the tab. You're right, though. It's a relief. I was beginning to develop a phobia about fortune cookies."

I pointed to his cookie. "Open yours."

He tore the wrapper open with one swift motion, leaving the cookie mere crumbs. Then, just as fast, he retrieved and held in between his thumb and index finger, the tiny white slip of paper.

"What's it say?" I asked, breathless.

He jerked once, coughed, and then read the fortune out loud.

"Rub your tummy if this food is yummy."

We erupted in a fresh wave of laughter.

Though I was still laughing, a motion to the side caught my attention. Sue Jan started to pass the booth accidentally on purpose and pretended to suddenly notice us. "Lovita? Have you been here all along? Monroe and I have been worried, just worried sick about you. In fact, I was on my way to the restroom to fish you out.

"And who are you?" Before the last word was out of her mouth, Sue Jan was batting her spidery lashes in Clint's face.

I picked up the fortune about my father and held it up.

"Excuse me," Clint said, sliding out of the booth, plucking the fortune from my fingers, and lifting his hat with the other hand. "I'd best be on my way."

He turned to Sue Jan and said, "I'm just a friend of the family." Then he threw one last smile my way. "An *old* friend."

Before she could open her mouth again, Clint Greech had disappeared. You had to hand it to the man; he knew how to make a quick getaway.

"Well, that was rude!" she exclaimed. "I never got the chance to meet him. Who was he?"

"Oh, just an old friend of the family, like he said," I answered, trying to sound nonchalant about the whole thing. But I knew there was no use trying to hide anything from Sue Jan. Resigned, I slid halfway out of the booth.

A sly smile crossed her brazen red lips. "Lovita, I know every pea-pickin' person in your family tree, and I don't believe I've ever seen that one before. Oh, I can see it all now. Clear as a bell in July."

"W–w–what?" I scrunched my face at her mixed-up expression.

"Women our age are supposed to look for younger men to marry to balance us out," she said, walking two fingers of one hand followed by two fingers of the other across the table. "Frankly, Lovita, I'm surprised that you haven't learned more from me." Her fingers continued walking, even sidestepping a pool of soy sauce spilled on the table.

"You're supposed to rob the cradle, not the nursing home." She demonstrated this thought by keeling the other two-fingered walker over on the table, then she commented, "Too old, he just couldn't keep up with you."

I tried sliding farther out of the booth, waving one hand to silence her, but she blocked me and kept on talking. "I've heard enough."

"I'm glad you're coming back to the table, or rather the table with the two hot guys. Monroe and I are sitting with them, and I gave them our number. I asked them for a double date. He's supposed to be keeping them busy while I look for you—I—I mean, go to the bathroom. So, Lovita, forget about the guy with the h–h–at."

Suddenly it hit her and Sue Jan came to a full stop. Her mouth kept moving, but nothing came out, which is unusual for Sue Jan, believe you me. I knew she'd finally realized who the man in the booth was. "The hat." She grabbed both my arms and squeezed hard. "He's the man with the Stetson, isn't he?"

I slid all the way out of the booth and dusted the crumbs off my skirt. "I'll tell you more later. Let's get back to the table. By the way, what did you find out from those guys?"

"Ahh, well."

"Sue Jan. I'll bet you never stopped talking. Am I right?" I demanded.

She started playing with the hem of her shirt. "Well, I wanted to, but they were so cute. You'll see. And you can talk to them yourself. The tall one has the cutest dimple, but the shorter one has a smile that'll melt your heart. I'm serious. You'll see."

Monroe, looking lonely and forlorn, sat at the table, which only moments before had been occupied by the two "hot" men.

"Where are they, Monroe?" demanded Sue Jan as we walked up to the table.

He stood up, and the napkin fell off his lap onto the carpet. "They left, Sue Jan." He continued trying to explain to the beat of Sue Jan's toe-tapping, no-nonsense expression: "They mentioned something about being tired and they left. It is getting late." He added with halfhearted but hopeful conviction, "Maybe they have to go to work tomorrow."

Poor Monroe. He had a lot to learn about Sue Jan.

To Bee or Not To Bee

Sunny Saturday morning began as usual with a pot of fresh coffee brewing. I set some bacon in the oven to cook at 350 degrees for 45 minutes. My mama taught me that little cooking trick. It's easier to cook bacon that way than in the frying pan. Besides that, all the grease drips off the rack into the shallow pan underneath.

Still in my robe, I carried a cup of coffee out the back door, now minus a screen, and sank into the quilt-covered swing. A call to the sheriff's office again produced no results. They were still busy dealing with the effects of the storm, but promised to come out and investigate soon.

Why'd I feel so tired? Then I thought about all of yesterday's happenings and figured that my body deserved to be tired after all that. Plus, Sue Jan and I had stayed up late talking. I had to catch her up on the letters and my meeting with Clint.

Savoring a long swallow of piping-hot coffee, I looked out over the yard. There were lots of branches and leaves still to be raked up. Maybe Sue Jan and I would get to it today. Then again—I shifted position and settled my back farther against the porch swing— maybe not. Sue Jan hadn't even gotten up yet, and she was sure to be cranky whenever she did. *Ring. Ring.*

Before I could get up, the ringing stopped. Probably a wrong number. I watched a hummingbird hover over a plumbago bush, the purplish-blue flower clusters in full bloom. My Bible was on the white wicker side table across from the swing, tucked behind some potted African violets and a small jade plant. I moved to the matching rocker next to it. Somehow it had weathered yesterday's storm without getting soaked. My fingers turned to Psalms, where I read a few chapters. The words of the thirty-fourth Psalm jumped out at me. "The LORD is near to those who have a broken heart."

I looked up at the ceiling dotted with spiderwebs and mud dauber nests. The porch ceiling needed a good sweeping with a stiff broom. We used to joke in my family that God was on the ceiling because that's where we always look when we pray.

"Lord, I'm in need of a coupla things," I prayed, looking up. "First, please help me find out what happened to my daddy and if he was, if he. . ." I sniffled back a sob. "Then help me bring whoever did it to justice.

"And, Lord, You know me better than anybody else. And even though Sue Jan is my best friend, Lord, I can't tell her the things I tell You. Please hear my prayer. I'm hurting right now, Lord. Sue Jan's always looking for Mr. Right, and I know I make fun of her a lot for doing it, but at least she's still looking. I've given up on ever finding a husband. And I pretend like I don't care, but I do. I want to get married. Maybe even have a baby."

I pulled a tissue out of my robe pocket and blew my nose. "But it seems so impossible, Lord. Nobody's going to fall in love with a woman like me. Men like skinny women. Well, most men anyway. Even Christian men who aren't skinny themselves like skinny Christian women. And I definitely want to marry a believer if I ever do marry. Lord, I know You are the God of the impossible. Your Word says that all things are possible to those who believe, and right now I need that kind of miracle, Lord. Please help me. Amen."

By the time I finished, my face was a waterfall of tears. But I felt good. At peace.

Slippered footsteps slid across the polished wooden floor of the kitchen. Sue Jan emerged from the door, wearing her favorite bunny slippers and a neon green shift. A bright pink scarf was wrapped tightly around her head, in striking contrast to the green of the Queen Helene mud-and-mint masque troweled across her face.

"Morning, Mama-Ita," she rasped before slurping from a large pink mug of coffee. She lowered herself by degrees onto the swing. "Ooh-wee. I'm tired," she declared. "You tired, too? Your eyes are all red."

Without feeling the need to explain, I nodded my head, and then drew a long comforting slurp from my own cup.

"That was Monroe on the phone." She paused to pull a loose thread off her gown. "He offered to drive us over to Bentley to order a new window for the shop and pick up new supplies. Says he's more than willing to do the remodeling for us himself—and for free."

"For free?" I asked, brows raised. "Oh boy, Monroe's got it bad for you, Sue Jan."

"Fell under the seductive spell of a bodaciously big, beautiful woman. True 'nuf," she commented without an iota of humility. Sue Jan smoothed both hands around the soft scarf on her head. She seemed extra satisfied with herself today. Monroe was in love with her, and she knew it full well. The woman would not hesitate to use poor Monroe to do her bidding and put up with all her nonsense. There was power in that.

I strummed my nails against the wicker side table, wondering if I should say what I was going to say. *Ra-ta-tum. Ra-ta-tum.* "Sue Jan, remember Bill Crass?"

Bill Crass, who'd been captain of the football team when we were in high school, was a brawny, barrel-chested guy, whose one ambition in life was to start up his own scrap metal business.

Sue Jan's head popped up like a prairie dog. "Now why would you bring him up, Lovita? You brought him up yesterday, too."

"I was just thinking. You know, about all the guys you've been in love with over the years."

She leaned forward to set her cup on the table. "I wasn't in love with Bill. I just liked him a lot. I was 'in like.'"

"Does he still manage that collision repair shop in Bentley?"

She nodded a yes and attempted a laugh. "Crass's Crash Shop. I guess he got his wish about wanting a scrap metal shop and all." She opened her mouth to add something but then just stared down at the floor a moment.

"Remember Valentine's Day?"

She looked up, eyes suddenly sad. "How could I forget?"

I smoothed out a paper napkin with my hands. "You and I spent all weekend making glittery red and pink paper hearts and little heart-shaped pouches to hold candy."

She interrupted. "I bought his favorite candy."

"Goobers," I replied with a little laugh. "You also found out his locker combination with a little help from my daddy's binoculars. I told you right then and there, 'Sue Jan, if the CIA ever finds out about your natural gift for spying, I'm convinced they will recruit you right on the spot.' "

She managed a giggle. "I got Earl the custodian—"

"To let us in an hour early with a wink and a box of doughnuts."

How Sue Jan found out about everybody's favorite food obsession was a mystery to me, but in his case, they were blueberry cake doughnuts. Earl was a happy man.

"Remember how we decorated Bill's locker with Christmas tinsel and those hearts we made?"

She nodded and plucked her cup from the table for another sip.

"If I recall, we glued a real pretty picture of you *from the neck up* inside one of them, and intertwined with that heart was a second one with a picture of Bill in his football uniform, glued in the center."

Sue Jan swallowed and pointed her spoon at me. "You remember how we hid out in Earl's custodian closet with all the smelly mops and dust pans across from Bill's locker. The door was open just a crack, just enough for a good view. The first thing Bill did, when he saw his locker, was stand there. I thought he was mesmerized by it." She bit her lip, and her jaw tightened for an instant. "But then he unzipped his backpack, ripped down all our decorations, and stuffed them inside. One quick zip."

"And it was all gone," I finished. "We went through four cartons of ice cream together before you got over him."

"But I did. The one that took me the longest to get over is Moss. Until Hans, that is."

That would be Moss Harvey, the traveling salesman who used to come through town about once a month. He sold restaurant supplies to Callie. Sue Jan knew his schedule and entire sales route in the tristate area by heart before she ever spoke a word to him.

"You really had it bad for him, Sue Jan."

"Have," she added, dumping another spoonful of sugar into her coffee.

"What happened to him? Did you ever find out?"

She stared at her coffee and stirred. "He gave up sales and moved to Alaska to work on a deep-sea fishing boat. That's the last I heard."

"Oh. Sue Jan." I paused. "But Monroe Madsen's a sweet, wonderful man and I believe he truly loves you. Don't toy with his emotions the way I think you're planning to. Please don't hurt him."

She tugged at the silver hearts dangling from her ears. "You worry too much, Lovita." Sue Jan tapped her chest. "I know Monroe's a nice guy and the last thing I want to do is hurt him, but if he's willing to carry my groceries into the house or drive me places and entertain me at nice restaurants, why shouldn't I take advantage of that? Just 'cause there's no thought of romance on my part, doesn't mean I can't hang out with him sometimes." She swatted her hands at a wandering bee trying to zero in on her coffee cup.

I squinted my eyes at her. "Monroe is the first nice guy who was ever interested in you, not the other way around. Though, for the life of me, I can't understand why." I held out my left hand and pointed to the ring finger. "Monroe would marry you in a New York second, and would likely be the happiest man on earth if you gave him that chance. But you're more than willing to string him along instead. I don't git it."

Several more buzzing bees showed up and spiraled in a holding pattern around Sue Jan's sugar-loaded coffee. She batted at them deftly with a rolled-up magazine and sighed. "Lovita, I am truly sorry for you. It must be so hard to watch men falling all over themselves to get to me—and you're just watching from the sidelines. I have Monroe calling me all the time and a dinner date with Hans Han Sunday evening, not to mention the two hotties I met in Cheng's last night."

I laughed out loud. Sue Jan was truly enjoying all the attention. I closed my Bible hard, stood up, and headed to the kitchen, humming a little tune along the way to make her think what she said didn't get to me. "The bacon should be ready now. I'll fry up some eggs to go with it." There was no way I was going to give

Sue Jan the satisfaction of the last word.

But Sue Jan wasn't finished yet. She followed me into the kitchen and sat down at the table. "How soon you forget, Lovita, that I asked those two good-lookin' men at the table next to us out for a double date. I mean, I could have just been thinking about myself, but *nooo*, who did I think of but you, Lovita."

I looked up from the stove. "And what did they say?" I asked, curious.

"Oh, it's practically a done deal. They're in oil, you know. One was Jerry, or John something, and the other one is Henry something."

I laid my hand down on the cool countertop, still holding the spatula. "And what else did you find out about *them*, Sue Jan?" I asked, toying with her.

She stared down into her coffee as if it were a mirror and stirred the rich, brown liquid round and round. "Well—not much."

I accented each word with the spatula, now raised in the air. "I always thought you had a natural gift for spying. But I guess I was wrong. You have the attention span of a hummingbird." I clanked some plates out of the cupboard. "Hmph, some investigator you'd make. I guess you only care if there's something in it for you."

Her mouth hinged up and down like a nutcracker a few times before she finally spoke. "I—I'm sorry. They were just so cute and all. Real cute. I like men in khakis."

"Yeah, I hear that kind of stuff a lot from you. You like men, period. In khakis, in jeans, suits, shorts, kilts, uniforms, and swim trunks."

"Well, why shouldn't I?" She lightly patted the mint masque on her face, probably testing to see if it was dry. "The man I'm gonna marry is out there somewhere. But I've thought about this a lot. It's a big world out there, and Wachita's a small place. What if my soul mate's in another country halfway around the world? How's he ever gonna find me?" Apparently satisfied the mint masque was dry, she smiled, and it cracked into permanent green smile lines.

"I tell you, Lovita, searching for a husband is a 24-7 job, especially for women our size. It's like looking for that Waldo fella in one of those books. I always find him eventually—just takes me a while. I aim to find a husband, too, if it takes the rest of my natural life." She slumped a little lower. "I just hope it happens before the springs pop out of my biological clock."

"That was a nice detour off the subject. You obviously didn't find out one useful bit of information to help out." I folded my arms. "And what was poor Monroe doing all that time?" I demanded.

Dabbing at the corners of her mouth with a paper napkin, she cocked her head to the side. "I'm not sure. He was kind of quiet and just commented a few times. He didn't say much, come to think of it."

"Great," I muttered sarcastically.

Sue Jan threw down the paper and lumbered out onto the porch with her coffee.

I was mad, too, and disappointed. Why couldn't she just let go of all this flirting and chasing after men all the time? When was she gonna get clued in to the fact that chasing men just makes them run? And the ones she chased ran pretty fast, too.

Just as the eggs were done and I slid them onto the plates next to the mound of crispy bacon, Sue Jan hollered from outside.

"Aaahhh!" She burst into the kitchen. "That stupid bee! He stung me, right on the face."

I rushed toward her, kitchen towel in hand, and pulled her hand off her face to examine the sting. That bee had stung her for true, on the cheek right below her right eye. It was red and already beginning to puff and swell. I could see that even through the green of Queen Helene.

With tender care, I slid the stinger out with the edge of my fingernail. Which wasn't easy with Sue Jan's tears getting in the way.

"Ouch. Ouch. Oh, it hurts so much. Please help me, Ita."

"Don't worry," I said, comfortingly. Reaching into the freezer, I pulled out a soft pack of green peas and brought them to her. "Here, hold these on your cheek to help the swelling go down." The picture of the peas on the package were a pretty good color match to the mint masque still on her face, minus the tear streaks. The pink scarf completed the circus clown look. If only Sue Jan could see what I saw right now—but I didn't have the heart to tell her.

"Ow," she cried. "Now I can't go to Bentley. My head's gonna be puffed up big as a bison."

I gave her a good swig of liquid antihistamine then pushed the plate of bacon and eggs her way. The true meaning of comfort food.

She perked up right away. "Ummm, this looks good, but where's the toast?"

I smiled. "Coming right up."

When Monroe arrived two hours later, Sue Jan didn't look nearly as bad as before, except that one side of her face was still swollen and irritated looking. It had puffed up so fast that the mint masque was stuck in her pores in that one area. She was okay, though, other than not looking her best.

Monroe wore a pale yellow planter's shirt and brown and orange plaid pants. Poor thing looked like a model for a nerd catalog. The man needed a makeover—bad.

I went into her bedroom to ask one last time if she wanted to come with us. But the answer was still no.

"I'm not going, Lovita." She held up a hand mirror and winced at the reflection. "What if Hans were to see me like this? I don't even want Monroe to see me." She touched the puffy side of her face while studying her reflection. "Ouch. . .no," she shook her head with conviction, "I'm not leaving the house today."

I dumped the fortune cookies from yesterday onto the bed. "Do me a favor then and take a look at the fortunes in these, will ya?"

She nodded and licked her lips. "Did Bo bring you these, Ita?"

"No exactly. I—I—" *Ring. Ring.*

"I'll git it." She reached for the phone.

I breathed a sigh of relief, and quietly ducked out of the room.

I could tell Monroe was disappointed about Sue Jan's not coming along, but the man was gracious to a fault. Though reluctant on my part, Monroe and I took off for Bentley in his old Chrysler convertible. The day was beautiful and bright, the air clean and fragrant. Storms do have a way of clearing the air.

"Monroe." I smiled to reassure him. "Thanks for doing this. You know I appreciate your help."

He blushed. "Oh, I'm happy to help out, Lovita. It's my pleasure, really. It's not like I was doing anything today."

"Still, you really wish Sue Jan was sitting here next to you instead of me."

His face flushed again. "Well, ah—"

Smiling, I continued. "You don't have to pretend. I know how much you like her and I'm glad you do. Monroe, you're perfect for Sue Jan, but she doesn't know it."

His mouth fell open. It registered crystal clear what was on his mind. Monroe turned off the radio and glanced my way for a second. "Lovita, can I tell you something?"

I shifted position in the cracked leather seat. This was going to be interesting. "Sure you can, Monroe."

"I–I've always loved her." His voice cracked. "She—she never much seemed to notice me, though, and it was frustrating."

"I'll bet," I added with complete understanding.

He continued. "So, I went away to school and then decided to get a job in Bentley for a while. It was close enough to live here in Wachita, and maybe catch a glimpse of her sometimes."

He fiddled with an air-conditioning vent as he

talked. "It's so hard to be around when she's flirting with other men. I tried to make my intentions clear, but Sue Jan—" His voiced stopped short. "I don't know."

"Monroe, I believe you are the best thing to ever happen to my best friend. Are you willing to do whatever it takes to win her heart?"

He swerved the car onto the shoulder of the country road we were still on. I was thankful that the road was clear of all traffic and potential onlookers, though, on my side of the road, a certain fenced-in cow seemed somewhat interested. Monroe turned to me, his expression somber and serious. "Short of breaking the law or one of God's commandments, I am."

To his surprise, I took his hand and shook it. "Good, then here's my plan. You and I are gonna make Sue Jan jealous. You pretend to be interested in me, and I'll do likewise and I guarantee she'll get a wake-up call to reality before it's all over."

"I don't know, Lovita," he said with a grimace. "Sue Jan might believe it. I mean, you're just as beautiful as she is and all."

My mouth dropped open like a trapdoor. "Why, Monroe, that was—that was sweet. You didn't have to say that." Now was my turn to blush. It was the nicest compliment I'd heard in a long time.

He went on. "It's true. Hasn't anyone ever told you that before?"

I looked ahead at the road. "Not for quite a while, Monroe."

A small gray car with windows tinted dark came up the road from behind and slowed as it passed.

Quickly snapping the conversation back to the plan, I suggested, "We'd better get going. There's a lot to do." If Monroe had stayed on this track a second longer, I would surely have liquefied into a pool of emotion right in front of him. And I wasn't ready for that. Not after wringing my heart out to God this morning.

10

THE CLUE-Y IN THE CHOP SUEY

A bustling town, Bentley was the same size as Wachita a few years ago. But throw in an anchor store like Wal-Mart, and wah-lah, other businesses crop right up alongside. Monroe and I headed first to the hardware store to order a new picture window for the shop, then we went straight to the beauty supply store. There was a sort of jittery feeling going up and down my spine, though.

"Monroe," I asked, "do you get the feeling that we're being watched or—or followed?"

He stopped in midstride and straightened. "Well, now that you mention it, Lovita, I have had kind of a funny feeling. But I couldn't quite put my finger on it like you just did."

We turned and looked back as if to catch someone following us freeze-frame. Kinda like that Stoplight game kids play. But everything seemed normal. Traffic moved as usual, and regular people crossed at intersections or waited at the bus stop. No suspicious characters anywhere. As we turned to walk into the shop, I thought I caught a glimpse of a small gray car passing by, like the one we saw earlier. I thought I saw a rental plate. But as I squinted for a closer look, it sped down the street.

With my beauty operator's discount card, I was able to purchase all the flatirons, curling irons, and blow-dryers we needed for a three-chair beauty shop. For good measure, I threw in some new brushes, combs, and curlers. The color and perm solutions had ridden out the storm safely in my supply closet, so we didn't need any. While Monroe loaded up the car, I browsed through the latest catalog of stations, chairs, mirrors, and lighting. Next to good food, these were the sorts of things that got me excited.

Jolene, the owner, marinated in musky perfume, approached me and leaned across the counter. Her hair, bleached and teased high, perfectly matched her eyebrows—a sort of bone color. I guess it looked natural—for a bone, anyway. I was glad she wasn't a walking advertisement for Lovita's Cut 'n Strut, though. Jolene did her own hair and was proud of it, but the pale color was a startling contrast to the orange of her "fake bake." An expert gum snapper, she popped and snapped seven straight times before she said a word.

"Lovita." She planted her index finger on the catalog. "That's what you need for your shop. It's time to freshen the place up." She puckered her fuchsia lips. "Last time I was there, it was looking a little dingy and 'small town' inside." She continued, "But then, maybe it's okay for a small town like Wachita. I wouldn't know about that since I live here in Bentley." She fluffed her teased hair. "No offense, mind you," she said, patting her ample chest. "That's just my opinion. My professional opinion."

"Oh, really?" I answered, annoyed by her uppity attitude.

But as soon as I turned the page, every iota of annoyance melted away. There on the page was everything I'd ever dreamed of for the shop. Light pink marble stations bordered in black marble, with drawers for everything and holsters for all the tools of the trade I just bought. And pink and chrome leather chairs. Real leather. It just so happened, too, that everything Monroe was loading into the car right now was pink and black. But how could I afford to buy the stations to match? Sue Jan was right about my financial situation. I was just breaking even. I closed the book and sighed deeply. Just a pipe dream. Maybe someday.

"You all done, Lovita?" Monroe came back into the store, panting. "What were you looking at?"

Jolene grinned wide to show off her capped teeth, eyes traveling up and down Monroe like an MRI. "And who are you?" she purred.

"M—Monroe Madsen."

A sudden recollection lit her eyes. "Haven't I—" She pointed. "Haven't I seen you before?"

"Well, I'm a lawyer here in Bentley."

She interrupted with a loud clap of her orangey hands. "Oh really? A lawyer? That must be how I know you. My son's always looking for a good lawyer. Got a card?"

Monroe handed her one. She took it then latched on to his hand, shook it, and pulled him in closer to her face.

"The name's Jolene—Jolene McNulty." She smiled. "Well, hmm, pleased to meet you, Monroe." *Pop. Pop.* She expertly chomped and squeaked a mouthful of pink gum. "Maybe we'll be seeing one another again real soon." She winked with brazen come-hitherness.

What a hussy.

I squeezed his arm a little and spoke through my teeth for emphasis. "Yes, thanks, Monroe, you've been such a wonderful help to me. We've really got to be going now."

As I ushered the confused Monroe near the door, Jolene yelled out, "Bye, Lovita! You come back and order those new pink and black stations, y'hear? That'll bring people into your shop. You'll see."

Once out the door, I leaned against the white brick wall outside. "Whew." I patted my forehead. "I thought she would never stop yapping."

"Pink and black stations?" he asked. "What's that?"

"Just a silly dream, Monroe. Now let's get going to the next phase of our trip. And FYI," I added, "her son's always looking for a good lawyer 'cause he's always in trouble with the law."

He nodded, eyes wide. "So, what's next?"

Spotting a certain place, three shops down, a fancy men's clothing store, I had an idea. An emergency make-over kind of idea. Monroe needed fashion triage, and this store was as good a place as any to start.

An hour later, and a lot lighter in the wallet, Monroe and I emerged with six bags of new shirts, pants, ties, socks, shoes, and even handkerchiefs. Although reluctant at first, the more clothes he tried on, the more he seemed to get excited about how he looked. I had to admit, Monroe cleaned up well, like a shiny new penny. When I was a little girl, my daddy showed me how to clean a gunky old copper penny with a few drops of Tabasco sauce. Cleaned the tarnish off like acid to reveal the bright copper underneath. Monroe was looking good. Except for his hair, which looked like a Chia pet somebody forgot to water. For a long time. A very long time.

We tried to jam and jostle the packages into the trunk, but decided to put the top on the convertible instead and leave the packages in the backseat. Although it was lunchtime and we were both starving, I promised Monroe we would eat right after the next errand.

But on our walk to the barbershop, we passed a little Hispanic church tucked in between the storefronts.

"Monroe?" I stopped short. "Do you know any Spanish?"

"Not much. Why?"

I drew up close to the church's signboard and pushed away a wisteria vine. A shower of fragrant grape colored blossoms landed on my shoe. *There.* Tacked on a cork message board was a large blurred photocopy of Sue Jan, or someone who looked remarkably similar, with a message under it.

"Can you read that, Monroe? My Spanish isn't very good."

He lifted his glasses away from his face and squinted up close to it. "Says something about a prayer vigil. No, it couldn't be for Sue Jan. Maybe it's for some woman who looks a bit like her, and the church is praying for some reason."

"Umm. . .maybe so," I answered. But I knew in my heart there was something more to it than that. It seemed as if Hazel and Inez had put the call out for prayer warriors in every church between here and the border. Maybe even beyond that. Sue Jan was on Hazel and Inez's "Most Wanted" Salvation Hit List.

The Barbershop Quartet was only half a block away. I knew the cutters there, and even though the name of the shop sounds kinda musical, the shop itself is not. You'd expect four barbers with waxed handlebar 'stashes, Johnnie's Follies hats, and garters on their shirtsleeves, singing turn-of-the-century ditties in perfect harmony. The four guys who own the shop can't sing worth a lick. They sure can cut hair, though. But one of 'em does happen to have a mustache and he was the one who was available to do a movie star makeover on Monroe's hair. Yippie dippie do.

First, Ed shaved and trimmed Monroe's sideburns. Then, under my direction, he slimmed and shaped the college-nerd/Chia-pet-gone-bad hair into a short, stylish cut. He gelled it a bit for volume and finished with a light spritz of manly smelling hair spray. When Monroe stared at himself in the mirror, he acted like he was staring at a stranger. I had to agree with him there; Monroe didn't look like himself at all. The man in the mirror was transformed. With a close shave and some moisturizer, Monroe's skin gleamed to match. The little man in the seersucker suit was gone, leaving a new Monroe, now officially transformed into a hottie.

Sue Jan was gonna be so jealous. And hopefully, she'd fall head over heels in love with the man.

Monroe couldn't stop thanking me, staring in amazement at his reflection in every shop window we passed. "Lovita, I—I just can't thank you enough. I feel like a new man. I feel confident for a change, and for the first time in my life, I—I think I might just have a chance with her. Do you?"

"Oh yeah." I smiled and gave him the thumbs-up. "But one more thing," I added, eying his dreaded round brown glasses. "Do you own a pair of contacts?"

"Yes. I have a prescription for disposable ones I dropped off, but I haven't picked them up yet."

"Before we leave town we're gonna pick up that prescription. Remind me, okay?"

I still had the nagging sensation that someone, somewhere, was watching us, hidden eyes boring holes clear through. But from where? I kept looking around as we walked.

Sammich's was on the corner. It used to be a five-and-dime drugstore and soda shop back in the twenties clear through to the sixties, but someone bought the owners out and expanded the lunch counter into a nice restaurant specializing in sandwiches. I didn't feel like a sandwich today, though.

We sat down and ordered the special: chicken-fried steak, mashed potatoes, and ham and green beans. *Yummy*. The waitress came to our table almost immediately with a steaming tray of food and iced teas.

We said a quick blessing and didn't talk much for the next few minutes. There was a lot of chewing and cutting and scraping of plates going on. I looked up for a second to get my bearings and noticed a familiar hat on the lunch counter. A TV blared overhead.

Clint Greech raised his hand in a brief salute. A coincidence?

"Uh, Monroe, I'll be back in a minute. I've got to go talk to someone. Don't let the waitress take my plate or anything, okay?"

Mouth full, he nodded.

Clint motioned to a stool, and I shook my head. "Stools and me just don't go together," I said over the TV news chatter.

He put a hand to one ear. "What?"

"I said, what are you doing here?"

Frustrated, he motioned to the waitress behind the counter to turn the sound down. She shrugged and held up the remote.

"Thanks!" His voiced boomed in the sudden silence.

The waitress popped a defiant bubble and turned away to wipe the counter.

"I've got some news for you, Lovita."

I rested an arm on the counter. "Were you following us in a gray rental car?"

He met my eyes with the same candor. "Yes to the first part. I followed you here. And you were plenty busy, too." His brows rose. "But not in a gray car. Was someone tailing you in one?"

I nodded.

He winked. "You're Clark's daughter, through and through."

He dug the heels of his boots into the lower rung of the stool, grasped his cup in one hand, and took a short sip of hot black coffee. "Well, I thought I should keep an eye on you in case whoever sent that fortune stirs up a hornet's nest. If your father was murdered, the person who did it won't be happy about that getting out. Promise me you won't go any place alone. Pay attention to your instincts. Okay?"

Ashamed I'd accused him of tailing me, I nodded sheepishly.

He set his cup down and handed my fortune back to me. "All right. Here's what I have to tell you. First, the fortune cookie messages we both received originated from the same place."

Leaning against the bar for support, I looked at the slip of paper and took a deep breath. "And?"

"Second," he continued, "both notes are printed on the same type of rice paper used for the printed fortunes inserted into fortune cookies. And, the paper originated in China. Believe it or not, there's a distinct watermark on the paper, invisible to the naked eye for the most part, but not"—he smiled—"under the microscope."

"So the Chinese fortune cookies are made in China. Is that unusual?" I turned the fortune over. The "lucky" numbers were printed in purple.

"Maybe, maybe not." He tipped the cup and swigged the last drop of coffee. "But I've discovered that most fortune cookies made in this country use American-made rice paper. It's cheaper than the imported kind. There aren't any fortune cookie bakeries nearby. The closest one is in Houston, and I already checked that one. Came out clean." Clint motioned to the waitress at the counter to fill his cup. "I'm sorry,

I should have already asked. You want one?" he asked politely.

I looked back with fondness at my food growing colder by the second. His plate now bare, Monroe waved a puzzled hello, which I returned, then he pointed at Clint. "No thanks, Clint. I should really get back to my friend and my food. Is there anything else?"

He gripped the cup with both hands, staring into it. "I figure the messages came from somewhere in Wachita, from someone who knew your father and me. I've been racking my brain, trying to remember if there was anyone with a grudge against us or a relative of someone we sent to prison—but nothing adds up. I can't tell you much about what Clark was working on before he died, but I can tell you that your father was investigating something big. I was out of town when he called. We were supposed to meet. . . ."

"But you never got to," I finished.

He nodded, gaze straight ahead. "I was suspicious from the start. But at the time, there was no evidence to the contrary." Clint rested his hand on mine. "Now it's not likely to come to this, but if I gather enough evidence, we may need physical proof that your father was murdered. Do you understand what I'm asking, Lovita?"

I swooned back hard against the counter, feeling like my heart had just been sucked into a black hole in the middle of my chest.

"You okay?" Clint held my shoulders. "What I'm asking is hard. But I need to know if you would be willing to sign an order to exhume your father's body for an autopsy if need be."

I began massaging my temples and managed a weak reply. "Yes, if it will help catch whoever did it."

Clint reached in his jacket, pulled out an envelope, and slid it down the counter. He gripped the Stetson with one palm. Tossing down a five by the bill, he nodded. "That's the consent form. I'll see you tomorrow. You can give it back to me then."

"Okay, but you know I go to church. Right?"

"I know. You're your father's daughter." He winked. "By the way Lovita, I've met some interesting people in Wachita."

I perked up. "Geologists?"

He smiled. "That's what they say."

My heart quickened. I remembered the conversation at the diner. "Callie Calloway runs the diner in town and she says there's something strange about those men. They're not who they say they are. She says we need to play it cool. Should I—should we be afraid?"

He tapped on the brim of his hat. "Not of them, Lovita. That's all I can tell you right now. Just trust me. I'll be in touch."

"Wait, I have one more question. I don't know if you can help, but I put a call in to the sheriff's office here in Bentley, about that message in my cookie, and they said they'd be sending someone out to investigate. But so far, no one's come by. Can you help?"

"I'll look into it and get back to you, Lovita."

With that, he was about to leave when something caught his attention on the screen above. "Waitress!

Can you turn that up please?"

She gave him a look that would melt steel, pointed the remote, and pressed the VOLUME button. A popular newscaster, hair plastered in place like a mannequin, read the news in the usual concerned baritone.

". . . weapons codes used for computer simulations of nuclear weapons tests—to data stolen from the lab at Los Alamos. . ."

In a blink, Clint was gone—so fast the swinging doors still paddled back and forth.

Monroe noticed my wobbly state and got up to help me back to the table. That's when the entire story began to spill out. I pushed the cold plate of food away, but I agreed to a cup of coffee. Then we had coffee and dessert, and I finished telling him everything.

"So that's what you and Sue Jan have been whispering to each other about. I wasn't quite sure about what all was going on. Just bits and pieces of it. Nothing really made sense. Of course, it wasn't any of my business, but thanks for including me." Monroe sighed.

I folded my napkin and placed it on the empty dessert plate. "We should go. It's getting late. Sue Jan's probably wondering what happened to us."

Monroe rose at once to pull my chair out. "You asked me to remind you about stopping to pick up the contacts on our way out of town."

"Thanks. You'll be glad we did." I turned to go.

"Lovita." He picked up the envelope and tentatively extended it to me. "You forgot something."

I forced a smile and took it. "Thanks." I rapped it

against my palm a few times before deciding to slip it in my purse. "Let's go."

Someone, for some reason, had decided to stir the stagnant waters in our little town of Wachita. And I'd stirred enough pots to know what would happen next. Something ugly was about to rise to the surface.

11

SZECHWAN, TWO, THREE

Sunday morning, I woke up early and fried up some chicken that had been soaking in buttermilk since the night before. Our church had a picnic at the end of every month following the service, and chicken was what I had volunteered to bring. *Ummm.* The coating was beginning to crisp up and brown to a rich mahogany. At first the kitchen, then the whole house, was permeated with the delicious smell.

I couldn't help thinking about what Clint had told me about Daddy. What did Clint suspect? Poison? Just the thought of agreeing to exhume my daddy's remains made me feel sick inside. *Lord, please help me. I want Daddy to rest in peace, but if he did not die a natural death, I ask that You help me find out who did it—in Jesus' name. Amen.* From that point on, I made up my mind to find the answer. Clint was right about my being Clark's daughter, through and through.

On the way home yesterday evening, Monroe and I hatched phase one of our plan to make Sue Jan jealous. Monroe would arrive here at 9:30 to accompany me to church, even though service didn't begin until 10:30. If I knew Sue Jan right, we wouldn't have to twist her arm to get her to come to church with us today. And she needed time to get ready.

Sue Jan stumbled into the kitchen, scratching her sides. "What time is it, Ita?"

Turning away from the stove, I said, "Good morning, Sue Jan. It's 9:00 in the morning, girl. You're looking good."

She yawned like a bullhorn and lifted the hand mirror left on the kitchen table from yesterday. I could tell right off the bat that the swelling had all gone away. Sue Jan looked like her old self again, except that her hair color was different.

"I like the way you colored your hair yesterday. I couldn't really get a good look at it last night, though. But it looks even better in the daylight. Real natural."

She swiveled her head like a sprinkler to show me her hair. "Warm medium brown with caramel highlights. I got tired of being a redhead." She sighed. "I just don't have the fiery temperament to match a color like that."

I bit my lip to hold back my truth-telling tongue from saying something I shouldn't. There was no way I was gonna mess things up.

Peering over my shoulder, she zeroed in on the pan. "Why're you frying up chicken, Ita? Smells so good," she said, smacking her lips.

"It's for the church picnic. Wanna come to church with me today?"

She sat at the kitchen table, scrunched up her nose, and opened the newspaper. "Well, I don't think so—"

"But I thought you promised Hazel you would go."

She must've shrugged, 'cause the open newspaper dipped up and down.

"Hey, did you find anything unusual in the fortunes yesterday?"

"Hmm? No," she answered behind the paper. "Bo dropped off a box, too, and she said that supplier was the Golden something or other. I cracked 'em open and looked at 'em all. None of 'em were like the ones any of us got at Chun's. Some had two inside, but other than that, they were same old same old. They tasted about the same, too."

"Oh," I sniffed. "Sooo, you don't remember the supplier's name?"

"Nah."

"You didn't answer me about church. Are you gonna go?"

"Uh, I don't think so, Ita."

I cleared my throat and tried to sound nonchalant. "Oh, that's too bad. Monroe's coming to pick me up at 9:30."

The paper floated down to the table. Sue Jan mouthed a perfect O, her chin tilted toward me for a moment. Shuffling over to the coffeemaker, she poured a cup into her favorite pink mug. In the meantime, I took the last piece of chicken out of the pan and set it to drain on some paper towels, then in the basket I was bringing to church. I set a heavy red and white checkered cloth on top.

She pulled out a kitchen chair with more noise than necessary and plunked down in it. "So you and Monroe had a good time together yesterday?"

I undid my apron and hung it on a hook behind the pantry door. "Umm-hmm."

"Umm-hmm," she mimicked. "What's that supposed to mean?"

"Is there any coffee left?" I asked to delay my answer.

"Huh? Oh, yeah, there's enough for one more cup."

I flicked off the coffeemaker, poured a cup, and fixed it the way I liked, with a touch of cream and three spoonfuls of sugar.

"So, Ita, what did the two of you do yesterday in Bentley?" In a state of exaggerated calmness, hands circling her warm cup, she smiled.

Eerie calm from Sue Jan is not a good sign. It means she's holding back a rising tide, and in Sue Jan's case, it was likely a tsunami. I had to be careful with the way this went. It wouldn't work if things were too obvious. She would smell a rat, for sure.

"We went to Jolene's and bought some blow-dryers, curling wands, and flatirons—all in pink and black—your favorite."

I was getting nervous. The regular Sue Jan would have squealed and clapped at this point. Instead, she merely nodded, a thin smile still on her face, like a plastic doll's.

"And—and then we went to a few other places, clothing stores and—"

Sue Jan lunged forward without warning. Her chest propelled the table forward, rocking a fourth of the coffee out of both cups. "He went shopping with you? Clothes shopping?"

Already busy wiping up the spill with my napkin, I frowned. "Yup."

She leaned back in her chair. "Sorry about that,

Ita, I didn't mean to."

"It's okay," I said reassuringly. "I already have too much caffeine in my system."

She tapped the side of her cup with the stir spoon, then she stopped and looked up at me. "Show me what you bought. Did you go to our favorite store, Luanne's? Did they get some new stuff in? I'd like to see what you got so I'll know what to borrow."

I soaped up a sponge at the sink to wipe down the messy table. As I wiped I whistled a little tune. "We didn't shop at Luanne's. We shopped for Monroe."

Her laughter and jiggling rattled the remainder of coffee out of our cups. I could have kicked myself for not bringing those cups to the sink first. Sue Jan was positively delirious.

"Aha, aha-ha-ha. Ahhhhh-ha, aha-a-hahaha. Didya go, didya go to—to the seersucker store, Ita? Aaaaah-ha, ahahahahahha."

"Sue Jan, stop that now," I ordered.

The brakes on her laughter ground to an abrupt halt. "What?" she asked confused.

I tapped my chest, implying matters of the heart were involved. "Monroe's my friend. Now granted, he's a new friend, but he's a real sweet guy, and we had fun yesterday."

I threw the sponge into the sink. "Now, if you'll excuse me, I've got to get ready for church. There isn't much time." I ran out of the room full speed, locked my bedroom door, and started changing into church clothes. Curiously, no banging on my door or lock jiggling followed. As a precaution, I had hidden the emergency keys, just to be safe.

The time in my bedroom seemed like an eternity. Dressed and ready to go in five minutes, I now had twenty-five more to kill, so I looked around the room for something to read. I looked through the letters again. Sue Jan and I had read them all last night, but the rest were just plain old letters Mama and Daddy had written to and fro when he traveled.

I passed in front of my dressing table. My face looked pale, so I pinched my cheeks. *Hmm.* Maybe a little makeup would help up the ante in this little game.

There were some samples from the shop I had been meaning to try. First, I dabbed on some sheer foundation and under-eye cover, then a hint of blush and dusting of powder in matte finish. Then a little eyeliner, mascara, and rose lipstick. I frowned. My eyebrows were too thin. Working with a brown brow liner and a tiny comb, I puffed them out for a fuller look. Pleased with the way my makeup had turned out, I flipped the curling iron switch and decided to add a few curls.

Just as I was doing the last section of hair, the doorbell rang. Monroe. Before I could unlock my bedroom door, though, Sue Jan beat me to the front door. Because I was in such a hurry, my hair got tangled in the curling iron and I couldn't get it out to save my life. So I ran to the door, trailing the cord behind. She was still standing there motionless when I joined her. And from this view I could see why. Monroe was a true monument to a makeover.

The man knew how to pay attention to detail once he learned how to do things right. His hair was fixed and styled the very same way the barber had fixed and styled it yesterday. And he was wearing the light gray suit I had picked out, with a starched pinpoint shirt and striped tie. Set your phasers on—stunning.

"Oh hello, Monroe," I said in welcome, holding out my hand to receive the bouquet of daisies he'd brought.

I noticed that Sue Jan was dressed up, complete with a charming straw hat festooned with tiny rosettes. She looked pretty.

"Sue Jan, Sue Jan," I said, snapping my fingers.

"W–what?" Her lips, painted and slicked in "Pouty Pink," barely moved. She was truly dumbfounded at Monroe's transformation. *Just as we planned.*

Monroe was positively transfixed. Sue Jan was, truth be told, a vision of loveliness. Maybe it was all the sleep she got yesterday. Not to mention all the extra care she had taken with makeup and clothes in such a short time. Although jealousy was a great motivation, would she ever truly fall in love with Monroe?

"C'mon in and set awhile, Monroe. I'll put these in water and be right back. . . . While I'm gone, why don't you tell Sue Jan about all we did yesterday?" I walked to the kitchen, trailed by the long, black electrical cord, but neither one of them noticed.

I said a little prayer as I arranged the flowers in an antique vase, bright green, edged in gold and hand painted. A prayer for Sue Jan and Monroe. For me, too. I had no idea how to untangle the curling iron from my hair.

12

Moo Goo Guy Trouble

The most imposing building in town, two stories with a carved scroll Old West storefront, A Bride Adorned Church had been there for years. Hazel and Inez were founding members. In fact, Miz Hazel's daddy had been the very first preacher when the building was brand new, back in the Stone Age.

These days, Pastor Meeks knew how to preach a good message, but lay things on the line as well. He taught that each person has to make a choice on this earth between heaven and a one-way ride down the hell-e-vator. Not that he says it in those words, exactly.

When we pulled up to the church, Monroe got out and opened the door, *first* for me as we planned, *and then* for Sue Jan. Of course she threw me a laser look, which told me one thing—our little plan was working out just fine.

As we walked up the steps, Sue Jan cut in front of me and took Monroe's arm, but he looked back at me and offered his other arm, which seemed to drive her crazy.

On the opposite side of the church, Clint Greech sat in a pew, Stetson in his lap. He'd taken more care with himself this morning. His wavy gray hair was slicked back, and it looked like he'd shaved extra close, too. Maybe too close. My guess is he forgot there were little bits of blood-daubing toilet paper in two places on his right cheek.

And there was a stranger in the middle pew. Looked to be in his thirties with dark shiny hair, sprinkled with a few grays—very few. Though he was sitting, I could tell he was tall, maybe six foot three or so. Good profile, too. There was a cute cleft in his chin. Brown eyes *with long lashes.* As if he knew there were eyes trained on him, he turned. Our eyes locked for what seemed like forever before I looked away. When I looked up again, I was horrified to see that *he* was still looking. He smiled and, to my surprise, I found myself smiling back. The mystery man had a set of beautiful white teeth. *Whew. I'm gonna need a fan.* This time, I broke the gaze and turned away.

A thin, energetic man, the worship leader held up his right hand to his right ear.

At this cue, the praise and worship team kicked into full-throttle worship. I looked over at Sue Jan and noticed she wasn't paying attention. She had already spotted the handsome stranger. She looked my way and instead of pointing to him, pursed her lips to the left so I'd look. To appease her, I glanced. To my relief, he was paying attention to the praise and worship. She gave me the thumbs-up.

The music began to wind down. Time for a "special" by one of the many talented singers in the congregation. Today Miz Hazel's granddaughter Bonita would sing. A beautiful young girl of eighteen, she chose an old hymn.

Sue Jan, who was still boring a hole through the mystery man, much to Monroe's dismay, suddenly began listening. In all the years I'd dragged her to church with me, I had never seen even a wisp of a tear or shred of emotion. But today I sat forward in the pew when I saw what I couldn't believe I was seeing. Tears.

That's when Pastor Meeks, a black Bible tucked under his arm, came out. In a low, soulful voice, he began to pray.

A quick glance revealed that Sue Jan was still paying attention. No faraway look in her eyes like all the other times. I had the feeling that something good was about to happen. My gaze lingered on Monroe, as well. He seemed intent on listening to the pastor.

Pastor Meeks began, "Who do you trust in your life?" He scanned the congregation. "Your husband, wife, family, friends, neighbors, boss, doctor, pastor?" He let out a short laugh. "I hope you trust that last one."

An immediate cacophony of *amens* reassured him that it was so.

"*Trust* is defined as 'reliance on another' or 'assured hope.' Proverbs 3:5–6 says, 'Trust in the Lord with all your heart, and lean not on your own understanding; in all your ways acknowledge Him, and He shall direct your paths.' Now, even people who you think are completely trustworthy may eventually let you down through circumstances beyond their ability to control."

He lifted an index finger. "God is the only One deserving of our total trust. He keeps His Word—always. He doesn't change His mind when He promises to do something, or tell you He doesn't feel like helping you today. We all know that with man, trust is not infallible. God is the only One who can and will totally keep His Word with us. . . ." Pastor Meeks balled up one hand and placed it into the palm of his other hand. "His Word is without fail. He *will* see it completed and fulfilled. He is the Author and Finisher of *your* life."

After about twenty minutes, Pastor Meeks closed with a prayer, and his Bible cover poofed shut.

The worship leader began to tap out a soft background tune on the piano.

"I noticed some new faces in the assembly today and others who have been with us a long time," Pastor Meeks began. "I ask you today, if you're sitting there in your pew and feel a stirring in your spirit because of the Word of God I spoke to you, I want you to know there's a reason you feel that way. God is calling you to be one of His own this morning. If you're ready to commit your life to Christ, I invite you to come forward now."

Bonita began to sing a soft background version of another old hymn.

"Excuse me, Lovita." I opened my eyes and looked up. Monroe was standing up. Stunned, I stood up and stepped into the aisle to allow him to pass. Before I knew it, he was at the altar. Sue Jan and I exchanged teary glances. I motioned for her to join him, but she shook her head.

As the service ended, on impulse I headed toward Clint to give him the consent form, but on the way, reached over to hug a tearful woman in the pew right in front of the mystery man. To my surprise, when the woman and I drew away, the mystery man, who had some sort of intoxicating citrusy aftershave on, reached forward and hugged me. A sudden tap on the back of my shoulder brought me back to reality and, though reluctant to do so, I turned. It was Clint.

"Lovita," he greeted me. "I saw you were on your way to say hello."

I gave him a hug and handed the signed form to him. "Are you staying for the picnic?"

He shook his head. "No, I'm flying out to New Mexico on some business."

I squinted. "Anything I should know about?" *New Mexico—where have I heard that lately?*

"Nope." Hat in hand, he turned and made his way down the aisle to the door.

Out in back of the church was a large meadow; a prairie expanse of grass, wildflowers, and trees. The church owned all the land behind for five acres, and there were no buildings or houses or anything but natural beauty in view. There were volleyball nets, horseshoes, and croquet areas set up, even special tables for checkers. Men were already congregating in these places. Picnic tables set in rows were covered with checkered cloths and some of the church ladies were in matching aprons, manning the serving line for the after-service stampede. We found a bench and set our things down, but no one was quite ready to sit except Sue Jan. I couldn't stop congratulating Monroe. His face glowed.

"I don't know why I feel so happy," he said, smiling.

Hazel leaned in. "That's the joy of the Lord, Monroe. Yessir—the joy of the Lord." She hugged Monroe hard and shook him. "Oh, I'm so happy you came to Christ. Son, what took you so long?" she asked.

Monroe laughed. "I guess I just never heard the gospel put quite that way before. Even though I've gone to different churches all my life, it was like I heard it for the first time. Do you know what I mean?"

Hazel grinned and patted his shoulder. "Yes, I know what you mean, son." She turned to Sue Jan with a wink and in her typical direct manner, asked, "Sue Jan, why didn't *you* join this handsome young man?"

Sue Jan was sitting on the bench, applying fresh foundation to her tearstained cheeks.

Gazing up at Hazel, she kicked the dirt with her shoe. "I don't know, Miz Hazel. I guess I just wasn't ready."

Hazel patted her head and encouraged her. "That's okay, baby, your time will come. I'm praying for you. So's Inez. And"—she began to walk off, muttering under her breath—"so's all of Wachita and Bentley."

I chased after her. "Miz Hazel? Can I talk to you for a minute about something?"

She reached down to pull up her knee-highs. "These things are always drifting." Then, with a big smile, she wrapped her arm around my shoulder and led me to a concrete bench by a willow tree. "I always have time for my girl."

We sat.

"What do you want, baby?" she asked, eyes dancing with joy.

"Miz Hazel, a couple of days ago, I found an old bunch of letters my parents wrote back and forth and I read 'em." I handed her the first two I'd read. Her eyelids trembled as she silently mouthed the words.

"I'm not sure how to ask this, so I'm just gonna say it. Was my daddy ever unfaithful to my mama?"

The light in her eyes waned. "Oh Lovita, my child. I knew one day you would ask me this." She shifted her legs on the cold, hard bench and slapped her knee. "Lord, give me strength." Hazel took a deep breath and looked at me. "Bessie Mae was a wonderful woman. One of my closest friends. But she had a jealous nature."

My lashes brushed up against my brow bone. I must have looked surprised or shocked, because Hazel touched my arm. A slight breeze rustled like crinoline through the tree branches above us.

"Inez and I didn't realize that about your mama at first. We were all three of us young and still wet behind the ears. We believed her story about Clark being unfaithful and went with her to confront him one day in Cheng's. I'm ashamed to admit that we accused an honest man. Your mama was heartbroken."

A leaf fell on my lap and I brushed it away, swallowing hard. It tore me up to ask the next question. "Miz Hazel, you don't think Mama could have—done anything to hurt Daddy, do you?"

Her face registered a tiny shock, and she took my hand. "Oh, no, baby. No. She was a spitfire when she was jealous, but I don't believe she ever would have done him harm. Perish the thought, child!"

Again, I swallowed hard. "Do you have proof that my father was innocent? How do you know he—"

She looked me square in the eye. "Because of this letter, honey. And because of his nature. Clark Horton was an honest, God-fearing man."

The tension seemed to melt right out of me. It felt good to know that my hero really was one.

"Thank you, Miz Hazel." I patted her hand and kissed it.

I caught up with my friends at the same table. Monroe wasn't ready to stand in the food line yet. He was still taking things in. Soon, he would have half a million questions.

"Sue Jan, you coming?" I asked.

But she was deep in thought. In all the years I'd known her, Sue Jan never once turned down the opportunity to eat or be first in line to get something to eat.

"I'll be along in a few minutes. You go on without me. I'll catch up." She forced a smile.

"What's wrong?"

"Nothing." She smiled again, waving me on. "Go ahead, I'll be there in a minute."

So, since neither of them was ready, I walked over and stood in line by myself.

Two teenaged boys walked past, their plates full. "Man, this chicken's good. I hope there's enough left for seconds."

A voice behind me said, "Me, too. That chicken looks delicious."

I turned around, then I tilted my head up to the

face of the gorgeous mystery man. Up close, he was better looking than I'd ever imagined. Tall, dark, and yummy.

"Well, ah, I hope you like it." I fumbled my words. "That's my chicken, the chicken I fried this morning, I mean."

He smiled down at me with that adorable smile. *And those eyes.* My legs felt weak.

"Then I'll be sure to love it. By the way, my name is Hudson Clark."

Two hours and a pile of bare chicken bones later, Hudson and I knew everything there was to know about each other. Well, almost everything. I felt a pang of guilt at ditching Sue Jan and Monroe; I noticed that Monroe was deep in conversation with Pastor Meeks. The questions had already begun. Sue Jan was flanked by Hazel and Inez. Sure enough, she had a plate of food. That was a good sign. A few other ladies sat nearby, as well, but she looked content enough.

But back to Hudson. He was an MK, a missionary kid, who'd grown up in Zimbabwe, though he had an adorable English accent. His family moved back to the States six years ago when his dad got sick with some exotic disease. No brothers or sisters, Hudson was an only child. Like me. A lawyer brand-new to Bentley. Moved in just yesterday. And he worked at the same firm as Monroe.

In my softest, sweetest voice, I asked, "Hudson, what brings you to Wachita?"

He coughed. "Since moving here, I mean not here, but stateside, I haven't really connected anywhere. I've visited a bunch of different churches, but it's difficult to find one I'm comfortable in."

"Why?" I asked.

"The mission field is so different. It's hard to find any place as satisfying to the soul."

Just then, Sue Jan came over and loomed in front of us. "Who's your friend?" she asked, batting her lashes.

He stood up, and she took a wobbly step back at his gorgeousness.

"Hudson Clark. . .and you are?" he asked, politeness personified.

"Sue Jan's my name. Hudson, eh? I like that name."

"You ready to go, Sue Jan?" I asked. It was two o'clock already.

She motioned to me. "Can we talk for a minute, Lovita?"

I set my iced tea on the table and smiled sweet as I could. "Will you excuse us?"

Sue Jan pulled me by the arm under the branches of a nearby sycamore tree, her face so close to mine, my vision blurred. "How'd you get to talk to that cutie-pie, girl?" She looked back at him. He was still looking our way and offered a cheerful wave. "He's something. Single, huh? Oooooh, Lovita, I'm happy for you and green-eyed jealous at the same time."

"Sue Jan," I answered, "honest, I don't know what he could see in me. I'm fat and plain looking and there's nothing special about—"

My personal put-down was interrupted by a loud, indelicate raspberry sound. "That's a bunch of hooey, Lovita!"

She grabbed me by the shoulders, her expression dead serious for a change. "Now listen up, girlfriend. You may be overweight, but you're not plain looking. Have you looked in the mirror lately? You must have redone your makeup or something, 'cause you're looking good, girl. And you're having a real good hair day, too. It's growing out fast and coming in thick. You been taking vitamins?"

Tears erupted from my eyes faster than I could stop them. "Oh, Sue Jan."

She continued, handing me her dinner napkin. "And as for you not being special—well, I better not hear you saying anything like that about yourself again. It's a lie and I just won't stand for it. You are the most wonderful, faithful friend, a kind person with the sweetest, most purest heart I ever did care to know. Got that?"

She poked my shoulder. "In fact, I hope that Hudson over there is good enough for *you*, not the other way around. Of course, if that were the case, I would be happy to take him off your hands."

"Oh, Sue Jan, I don't know what to say. I never knew you felt that way about me."

She kicked the dirt with one foot. " 'Course I do. I'm your bestest friend, aren't I?"

We hugged, and I noticed that my tears left a mascara smudge on Sue Jan's shoulder. "My masc—"

She waved me off and started walking back toward Hudson. I followed, perplexed.

"Hi. Sue Jan and I have to go, she's having a dinner guest over, a date—"

"Oh, that's too bad, Lovita," he cut in. "I was going to ask you out for some ice cream."

A low moan escaped my mouth. *How could I miss this chance?*

Monroe overheard and approached. "Hudson, right? I think we were hired the same day." They shook hands. "Hold on a second. Lovita, I would be happy to drop Sue Jan off so you two can go out for ice cream."

I lifted my shoulders, as if giving up to circumstances beyond my control, though I was delirious with joy. "Okay then, I'll go."

Hudson returned the smile. "Good, then it's a *date*."

I don't know why he didn't see it, but I'm sure at the sound of that word, I melted into a puddle right there in front of him.

Jalapeños, Heel Comets,
and Hans Han

Still walking on air from my ice cream date with Hudson, I came in through the back door instead of the front and danced into the dining room. Tiny red paper lanterns decorated with hand-painted parasols were swagged in rows across the ceiling. My crisp white linen tablecloth, starched to rigor mortis, covered the dining room table. Sue Jan's best china, rimmed in real gold, was set in two places, with my grandma's silverware and crystal goblets to boot. *And real linen napkins?*

"Sue Jan—Sue Jan, where'd you get those red linen napkins and how'd you get them to stand up like that?"

She stuck her head out of the kitchen. Beads of perspiration clung to her forehead and stray wisps of hair drowned in them. "What?"

"The napkins," I repeated.

"Oh, those, I bought them about a year ago when we went to that mall in Pearland. You know I've always been partial to red. It's such a romantic and powerful color. The color of passion." I don't know whether her face blushed or was flushed from the heat of the kitchen.

"I folded them into swans," she added. "Like that origin-namee. I got a book about that stuff at the library that showed you how."

"Ohhh-weeh. Well, it sure looks good." I walked over to the table. "And you even bought roses." I leaned over to sniff.

"I didn't buy 'em. Bo brought me some out of her mother's garden. Ain't they pretty? She brought 'em over with the. . ."

"The what?" I asked. My ears pricked up immediately. Something didn't smell right, and for once it had nothing to do with Sue Jan's cooking.

"And they smell good, too."

"Back up, girl." I pressed, "Now, one minute you were saying—"

"Oh, never mind that," she said, wringing her hands on the tiny, tasseled apron she was wearing. "Now Lovita, come on over into this kitchen and help me." She brushed a lock of hair from her face and ducked back into the kitchen.

I shrugged my shoulders and followed her into the other room, where I found her chopping carrots at reckless speed.

"I'm losing control," she said. "Things are messing up. I'll never get everything done and look presentable before Hans gets here."

I grabbed the knife from her hand. "Sue Jan, I don't want to see you lose a finger. What do you need me to do besides cut these carrots?" I asked, glancing down at a slip of paper on the counter. "What's this?"

"Well, for starters, how about—Give me that!" she

screeched. She snatched the paper away like we were playing spoons, our favorite card game, before I could pick it up.

"Who has handwriting that neat and precise?" I asked, puzzled.

"Lovita, that's a grocery list, a plain ole grocery list. I asked Bo to go and—and pick up a few things for me." This time Sue Jan began winding the satin apron strings around her fingers like a nervous jervous. "You know how frazzled I get. She just helped me out. You know, friend-to-friend and all."

"Hmmgh," I heaved. "No, your handwriting looks like something one of your cats wrote with her own tail. Not like this. Something's up."

"Lovita, I—I just don't have time for this. Now"— she stomped her foot—"are you gonna stand there accusing me of God only knows what or. . .or help your friend in need? Maybe Bo's a better friend to me than you are these days."

Aghast, I backed into the kitchen counter, felt something wet through my shirt, and whirled around. The end of the counter had a sizable soy sauce spill. I twisted the back of my shirt around front for a better look. "Awwh, Sue Jan, you're so crazy messy when you cook. Cain't you wipe the counter? How long does *that* take? Keep your wok area clean, that's what I always say, but do you listen? Nooo."

I plucked a kitchen towel off the counter, wet it, and began swiping at the stain before I realized the towel was coated with tempura batter. "Sue Jan!" I threw down the dish towel, grabbed the sides of my head, and let out a little yell.

"Tee-hee, tee-hee-hee," Sue Jan giggled, her body shaking.

"What are you giggling about?" I asked, defiant.

She giggled out of control. "You said, 'Keep your *wok* area clean.' I know you didn't mean to say that, Ita, and that's why it's so funny. 'Keep your wok area clean.'" She slapped the countertop in the throes of a laugh, but the counter was covered in tempura batter, which splattered every whichaway. Now it was my turn to laugh.

"My makeup, my hair! Oh, noooo, Lovita. What am I going to do? There's no time for this." She pulled a compact out of her apron and began dabbing the splatters off her face, hair, and clothing.

Meanwhile, I filled the sink with hot, soapy water and began sponging off the countertops and cabinets. The splatter had gone everywhere. In fact, sauces, egg whites, pieces of chopped vegetables, oil, and Lord-knows-what was all over the kitchen. Even on the top of Kitty-Mingus's head. She purred her annoyance when I wiped her head down. "Sorry."

Turning to Sue Jan, I pointed the sponge at her. "Now, back to what you said—I cannot believe you said that, Sue Jan. That was rotten, just rotten." I stiffened my back against the kitchen wall in a caustic mood. "Well then, what can *I* do for you, Sue Jan?"

Her forehead furrowed a moment. "Refresh me, Ita. What did I say?"

"You know exactly what you said. You said that Bo was a better friend than me." I volleyed it back at her in true Perry Mason fashion.

Surprisingly meek, Sue Jan sniffed. "I'm sorry. Now, if you want to move back up to the top friend position, here's what I need you to do. For starters, you can get all the ingredients together for the kung pao chicken so I can stir-fry it real fast."

Dumbfounded, I slammed the sponge into the soapy dishwater. The café curtains took the brunt of it. Hands on hips, I glanced around. "Well, where's the recipe?"

Again, that worried look. "D–don't you concern yourself with that, Lovita. I'll tell you what to get ready. Just follow my instructions, okay?"

"Why can't I—?"

On the verge of tears, she cried out. "Are you gonna help me or not? I've still gotta shower and get all fa-fa she-she, which will take even longer now that I'm mucked up with tempura batter. I don't blame you for that, but you owe me."

"Owe you? I don't believe my ears, but nothing you say these days comes as a surprise to me. Nothing. I'll help you, but this is the last time—"

"Goody," she interrupted with a clap. I saw her out of the corner of my eye, peeking at the little slip of white paper in her hand. "Kung pao chicken. The first ingredient is. . ." She began reading them all off to me, one by one, a little too fast for my hands to move.

4 boneless, skinless chicken breast halves (about one pound)
1 egg white

1 teaspoon cornstarch
1 teaspoon soy sauce
½ teaspoon salt
dash of white pepper
1 green bell pepper
1 medium onion
1 tablespoon cornstarch
1 tablespoon cold water
1 tablespoon dry white wine
½ teaspoon sugar
¼ teaspoon sesame oil
2 tablespoons vegetable oil
1 clove garlic, crushed
1 teaspoon finely chopped gingerroot
2 tablespoons hoisin sauce
2 teaspoons chili paste
1 tablespoon of a secret ingredient
½ cup chicken broth
½ cup roasted peanuts

"Check and check," I said. "Got it all, Sue Jan, except for the secret ingredient. Why are you hiding that recipe from me?"

"Oh, 'cause I'm going to add in the secret ingredient myself. It *is* top secret, you know."

"Why?" I asked narrowing my eyelids. "Why are you hiding that recipe from me? What's soooo secret about it? It's a recipe for goodness' sakes. You're acting like Hans Han."

"What do you mean, Lov—" Sue Jan was nervous. There was no hiding that.

"You know exactly what I mean." A sudden insight exploded in my head. Like a flash of light. "Ohhhh." I paced back and forth, excited at the thoughts swimming in my head.

Sue Jan followed me. "What, what Lovita? You don't need to think. You just need to roll up your sleeves and cook."

"Something's already cooking here." All of a sudden it all made sense. The roses and Bo's visit. "Ohhhhh." I grinned wide and white, like I'd just won the sweepstakes.

Sue Jan followed behind, now in tiny baby steps. She warbled with breathless anxiety. "It–it's not what you think, Lovita."

"How do you know what I think? Gimme that." I snatched the slip of paper right out of her hand. "Ha! Hahahaha." I twirled around, laughing. "Just as I thought. You got Bo to steal Hans Han's recipe for kung pao chicken. You little sneak."

"No. No, it's not what you think. It's not like that. She just borrowed—"

"Nice try, Sue Jan. But I don't ever remember you making kung pao chicken before, and you told him you made the best. You're scamming Hans with his own secret recipe."

She slammed her palms down on the counter and swiveled back with dramatic force. "Okay, Lovita, you got me. But I didn't have a recipe for kung pao chicken. You're right. I never made it before in my life. So Bo offered to help me out. It was her idea, too. If I don't make good on what I said, well, Hans won't trust me."

"*Trust* you!" I bent over laughing. "Wait, let me get this one straight. You stole Hans's recipe to make him believe that your recipe, which is in fact *his* recipe, is better? You're lying to Hans so that he'll trust you? Did I get that straight?"

"I know—I know." She shook her head, at the point of tears. "I just needed an excuse to invite him to dinner. Dating a man like Hans was just a dream before. He's so cute and all. And now that it's finally coming true. . ."

"Why Hans?" I asked. "Honestly, I don't know what you see in him, Sue Jan. He's such a cold fish. He doesn't have a personality. No sense of humor. He's sort of boring. What about Monroe? He really likes you. Always has. And he's nice."

"Monroe's just. . .Monroe," she said with a shrug. "He's nothing special to look at and he wears seersucker suits. And he's husky-sized. He sweats a lot, too. C'mon, Lovita."

"What about his makeover? You have to admit he looks good."

She massaged her temples. "Oh sure, he looks good today, but I haven't forgotten that just a few days ago he was the king of the nerds. Who's to say he won't revert back to his old self during the full moon? Like some kind of nerd werewolf."

"Trust me, Sue Jan, Monroe is transformed for good. He won't ever go back to the way he was." *Wink. Wink.*

She blinked back, eyes ablaze with sarcasm. "But Hans is cute, Ita, and he didn't even need a makeover.

He was born cute. I've always dreamed of dating someone good-looking who wouldn't mind dating someone like me."

"You mean someone fat," I clarified.

Tears dripped down her face, ruining what was left of her makeup. "Fat like me." Sue Jan plopped down hard on a kitchen chair. She buried her head in a kitchen towel, crying. "I love food, Lovita, but I hate being so fat."

"Fat like me, too. I know how you feel, but I don't think Hans Han, as good-looking as he is, is worthy of you. You have more personality and more good qualities in your little toe than he has in his entire muscular hottie body."

She let out a tiny laugh in between sobs. "It's a fat little toe."

We laughed and hugged one another. "I guess being fat isn't so bad if your best friend is, too."

"Or fatter," she added.

"Who you calling fatter?" I asked. "I am not fatter than you! Break out the scale, sistah. You challenging me?"

"I'm just kidding, sistah-gurl. That reminds me, Ita, I'm sorry about what I said before. You're my bestest-estest friend in the whole wide world, maybe even the universe."

"I know, Sue Jan. Same here. So"—I held up the recipe—"let's get started."

She glanced up at the kitty kitchen clock. "Oh, no. I'm running out of time, Ita."

"Don't you worry." I grabbed the apron off her and

tied it on me, waving her away. "I'll take care of the kitchen. You get ready. . . . Besides, that kitchen towel you just cried in? It must've had some kind of mustard sauce on it, 'cause it's all over your face."

She grimaced, took a few steps, and paused at the door. "Ita, you're gonna be my maid of honor."

"Well," I said, smiling, "I'd better go dye my pumps, then."

"Oh, Ita." She walked off, tittering.

I called to her. "Hey, what's the secret ingredient?"

She laughed. "Plain old jalapeños. Finely chopped."

"That's it? I was expecting something exotic."

Sue Jan tittered some more and disappeared down the hall.

I lined up all the not-so-mysterious kung pao ingredients, put the rice in the steamer, then rolled the egg rolls and deep-fried them ahead of time. Sue Jan could heat them up easily right before Hans arrived. The egg drop soup was ready, too. I chopped some green onion to garnish the bowls, and then spooned up a taste of soup for myself. Good stuff. Ummm. Hans was sure to like that.

I almost felt guilty for the little scheme Monroe and I had cooked up to get Sue Jan jealous. But I had to go through with it now. Monroe was counting on me.

"What do you think, Lovita?" Sue Jan posed at the doorway in a large silken kimono, her hair Chinese-ified and decorated with little paper parasols. Her lips were red and shiny, and her eyes were raccooned with liner and mascara in stark contrast to the pale makeup and powder caked over her face.

"I hate to tell you this, Sue Jan, but I think kimonos are more Japanese than Chinese. I could be wrong, but I don't think so."

A look of panic washed across her face. "Japanese? You're kidding. But red is a good color for me, and it's made of pure silk. I bought it off the Shopping Channel and it cost lots of money. Trust me." She shrugged her shoulders. "I guess I can't worry about that now; there's no more time. Hans will be here in just ten minutes."

"And you know he'll be right on time," I said.

"You think he'll notice?" She seemed worried.

A truthful, yet kind answer still swimming around in my head, I was saved by the doorbell.

"It's Hans. Oh no, not yet, Lovita. He's early."

"Wait a minute, Sue Jan," I said, looking down. "You have a heel comet on your shoe." She had trouble looking down past her kimono, but sure enough, a seven-square tear of toilet paper followed her every step.

"Take care of that while I get the door for you," I ordered. I undid the apron and ran my fingers through my hair. Heels clacking across the wood floor, I yelled back to Sue Jan as soon as I opened it, "It's okay, Sue Jan, it's Monroe!"

She popped her head out from behind the kitchen door. "Monroe?"

"Sue Jan," he ventured.

"What are you doing here?" she asked rudely. "I can't see you, Monroe. My *date* will be arriving any minute now. Now, I know it's hard for you, seeing as you like me and all, but—"

Monroe blinked. "Well, actually—"

"Tell him, Lovita. Hey, and you had better make yourself scarce, too. I appreciate all you did for me. Now scoot."

"For your information, Sue Jan, Monroe is not here for you. He's here for me. We're going on a date."

She stiffened. "A date?"

"That's right, a date."

She yanked me back into the kitchen and squinted in my face.

"What are you talking about?" she asked in a stage whisper. "I thought you were infatuated with your new boyfriend, and Monroe was infatuated with me."

The Academy would have been proud. I stared at her, at the ceiling, at my shoes. "He was, Sue Jan. No doubt about it. He was. B–but you're sending a clear message that there's probably no chance with you, and well, the man has to go on with his life. I'm single. He's single. And I can't count on it working out with Hudson. A girl has to make the most out of every opportunity."

"I can't believe you would go out with Monroe. You don't even like him like that."

With just a sliver of jealous defiance, I answered. "What do you care? You're just using him anyway. Besides, I happen to like seersucker."

She rapped my head with her tasseled fan. "Lovita," she said, staring right through me, "there's something not right about this. If I had time—"

Ring.

"It's the doorbell. Oh no, this time it *is* Hans." She motioned for Monroe to run into the kitchen. "You two go out the back door, and Lovita, on your way out"—she handed me the matches—"light the candles on the table."

"Coming!" she hollered in a pleasant tone. Then she swished at us with her hand and hissed, "Now go."

"I'll get the car, Miz Lovita." Monroe smiled, playing his part well.

Voice louder than usual, I said, "Oh Monroe, you silly boy, call me Lovita, or Ita, or Lovey! Take your pick!"

He tipped his baseball cap. "I'll get the car, then— Lovey."

I heard Sue Jan, on her way to the front door, blow a raspberry on her arm in response.

As I lit the candles, I said a little prayer. "Lord, You know Sue Jan and Monroe belong together. I don't know how You're gonna pull this one off, but I'd appreciate whatever You could do." I tippy-toed to the dining room door and peeked around the corner to look and listen in.

"Hans, my, my, don't you look all handsome." A black silk shirt, embroidered with a Chinese dragon and paired with black dress pants, clung to his muscular body. Hair slicked back, nails perfectly groomed, he reached out to grasp her hand and kiss it. Then he handed her a single long-stemmed rose—pink, not yellow, which was Sue Jan's favorite color in a rose.

"Now, Hans, why don't you have a seat in the front room? There's a nice breeze working through it this evening, and I'll get you something to drink if you like."

"No, thank you, Miz Sue Jan."

"Sue Jan, please." She tapped on his hard chest with her fan. "No more Miz. Just plain old Sue Jan, okay?"

"As you wish, M—, I mean, Sue Jan," he answered.

"You're sure you won't have some hot or iced tea, or a cola, or mineral water?"

"Mineral water would be acceptable, thank you."

Swaying playfully from side to side, Sue Jan asked, "Do you like my outfit, Hans? I bought it with you in mind." But before he could answer, Sue Jan made a silky-swishy exit into the kitchen. I popped my head back and squished up against the dining room door so she wouldn't see me. Ice cubes plinked into a glass.

Holding my breath, I peeked out again as Sue Jan came back out of the kitchen. She glared at me, stuck out her tongue, and held up a fist. That was a universal language that needed no deciphering.

Bearing mineral water in a crystal glass with a thin slice of lime, she handed it to Hans.

"You just make yourself comfortable. Dinner will be ready before you can say HongKong—KingKong—Won'tBeLong."

I slipped out the back door and caught the eye of Monroe, who was sitting in the front seat of the car. With a sly wink, I gave him the thumbs-up.

14

TWO FOR LOBSTER KEW?

Monroe parallel parked the Chrysler near Chun's, and when he opened the door, I realized from the look on his face that Monroe was sad. He was just going through the motions, all the while thinking about Sue Jan and Hans Han on their "date" back at the house.

We took a few steps toward the restaurant, and I stopped short on the sidewalk. "You know, Monroe, I really don't feel like eating there tonight. The thought of lobster kew, the dish I was planning to order, just doesn't appeal to me. Besides, I felt a little queasy last time I ate Chinese."

"After Cheng's?"

"Yeah."

Monroe looked down the street to our left. "If you don't want to eat at Chun's, where do you want to go?"

Down the street in front of Callie's, a van pulled up and four men got out. Part of the khakis crowd. I smiled. "Monroe, my friend—follow those khakis."

The bell on the door tinkled as we entered, and Callie shot me a knowing look. Without moving her head, she shifted her eyes to the right like some kind of Kewpie doll. I followed her direction—to my left. "C'mon, Monroe, let's get a booth over here," I motioned to a booth next to the men in khakis.

As soon as Monroe and I finished eating, I worked up all the nerve I could muster to swivel myself around and say hello.

"Well, hello neighbors," I greeted, cheerful as all get out.

The four men in the booth looked up from their plates, then at one of the men sitting on the end, then back to me. All appeared to be in their thirties—clean-cut with short cropped hair, fresh shaven, too. Three had dark brown hair and one, blond. It was obvious by the way they kept looking at him that he was the boss of them all.

Blondie, the apparent leader of the pack, cleared his throat with a *harrumph*, and was real careful in the way he wiped his mouth with his napkin. As he stood up to extend his hand, I could tell that smiles did not come easy to his chiseled face. "Well, hello neighbors yourself," he replied with forced cheer.

I touched a hand to my chest, you-Tarzan-me-Jane style. "I'm Lovita Mae Horton and this is Monroe Madsen." Monroe caught on real fast and said a real friendly hello. For a moment, just a split second in time, I mentally downloaded Sue Jan's technique for batting her eyelashes in a flirtatious way, and mimicked it as best I could. "And you are?"

"I'm, ah, Bob Smith and this is my—harrumph— geological survey team." He pointed to each man as he introduced him. "This is Jeffrey Clark, John Johnson, and Henry Rogers."

Smith sat back down, this time on the edge of his seat. He seemed uncomfortable, and I couldn't help wondering why. Monroe and I exchanged knowing looks.

We said hello to each one of the men, and I decided to test things out a bit. "So, Bob, where are you all from and what brings you to Wachita?"

Smith coughed. "From, er, Houston and we're geologists." He reached for the butter, and one of the men tried to help. The butter knife clanked across two plates while three of them bumbled around for it.

"Geologists, really? You must be looking for oil, then. I never thought Wachita had any. At least that's what the old-timers in town always said." I turned my attention to one of the others. "Jeffrey, are you from Houston as well?"

Johnson elbowed him and he looked up. "Oh, uh, not originally. I'm from Wisconsin."

"Where all that yummy cheese comes from?"

"Yes," he said, smiling.

I nodded. "Cheese. . .good stuff."

"I'm a fan," Monroe agreed. He pointed to his midsection. "But sometimes I can't handle it—lactose intolerant."

Feigning interest, Smith bit his lip. "Really."

"Yup."

The conversation was becoming downright painful until Callie showed up to rescue us. "You boys want some of my peach pie?"

The men all looked at the man called Smith, who answered for them. "No, I'll pass." The rest shook their heads in agreement.

"No thanks."

"Not for me today."

"Thanks."

I held up my hand. "We'll have some, Callie. You boys don't know what you're missing. Callie makes the best peach pie there is. She gets her peaches from Miller's farm."

Callie was quick on the uptake as well. "Hey, isn't that where you guys are staying?"

Henry Rogers immediately started choking on his water. I reached over to pat his back. "That's okay— Henry—is it?"

He nodded, still choking.

"Just the other day, I had a similar incident happen to me. Monroe here is good with the Heimlich. Aren't you, Monroe?"

"Sure am, Lovita," he agreed.

No one noticed Callie's brief disappearance until she returned with a tray of peach pie. "I decided to give everyone peach pie on the house tonight." Quick as lightning she had a plate under everyone's nose before he could sneeze. "You want it à la mode? I got some homemade vanilla ice cream in the freezer."

"I do, Callie," volunteered Monroe.

"I'll be right back, then. The rest of you enjoy."

Bob was just taking his first bite of pie when I decided to ask him something.

"So, what kind of rocks are you fellas looking at and all?"

He swallowed the first flaky bite, and for a second an expression of bliss passed across his face. "Just doing some fieldwork."

I patted the corners of my mouth with a napkin.

"Like you said, we're looking for oil. We think there might be a pocket or two around here." He cleared his throat again.

I continued the questions, propping the window of opportunity open as long as possible. "So how'd you fellas fare in the twister? I heard it blew over one of your trailers."

Callie returned with the ice cream and topped off Monroe's pie. She winked at me.

"I–it's fine, just banged up a bit. We caught the edge of the storm, that's all."

"Was anyone hurt?" Monroe asked.

"No, we evacuated before the storm hi—"

My cell phone started ringing right then, and I held up my index finger. "Excuse me for just a moment while I take this call."

"Hello?"

A hushed voice began, "Lovita, it's me."

Monroe threw me a look of concern and mouthed a question. "Sue Jan?"

The khakis crowd saw this as an opportunity for a hasty exit and slid out of the booth lickety-split.

"Hold on." I pulled the phone away from my face. "Bob, you boys leaving? Monroe and I were looking forward to talking with you some more."

He answered fast, fumbling with the bills in his wallet then layering them in the pay tray with the bill. "Oh, I know, but, well, we have to get an early start tomorrow to look for some more *rocks*, so it's best that we turn in for the night. But it was nice talking to you." By the tinkles of the bell on the door, I could tell that the others were already outside. Before I could say anything, Smith, now standing by the booth, made like a caboose and followed them out of the diner.

I plastered the phone back on my ear. "Sue Jan. You still there? Why are you calling—aren't you and Hans having dinner? And why are you talking so low? I can barely hear you."

"I'm in the bathroom." Her voice cracked. "Hans is getting married to somebody else. Says he's in love." Muffled tears escaped.

Somehow I knew Sue Jan was drying her tears on my fancy new shower curtain.

"Oh, honey. I'm so sorry." I tried to comfort her.

She continued sobbing. "And her name is Soon and she's supposed to be here in a couple of months. It's an arranged marriage, but he's crazy for her. Met her in China, and I bet she's skinny and pretty."

"Where's Hans, honey?"

She paused then started hiccoughing. "I guess he's still out there. We h–had dinner and h–he loved it. Said the kung pao was 'sue-perb' and he even asked for the recipe."

I snickered. "Oh that's too funny."

Sue Jan, however, was too caught up in the throes of Han's rejection to see the irony.

"I just couldn't face him after he told me. It hurts—like a mule just kicked me in the stomach. Ohhh, what'll I do?"

I looked at Monroe. "You hang tight, and we'll be right over. Dry your eyes, splash some cold water on your face, and tell Hans you're not feeling well. Maybe he'll take the hint and go home."

"O–okay, I–Ita," she sobbed. "I'll do it. Hurry."

It almost broke my heart, hearing Sue Jan that way. Monroe and I hauled out of the café. Sue Jan needed our help.

15

EGG FOOL YOUNG

The Chrysler roared into the crunchy gravel in my driveway, followed by a squeak of Monroe's brakes, which I guessed needed mechanical attention.

Monroe, forehead creased with worry, jumped out of the car, forgetting his usual manners. He disappeared into the house, but I could track his progress by watching the lights flick on in all the rooms. I unhooked the seat belt and lifted the door handle. Arrgh. Just because I wanted to get out the car door fast, it was stuck. Pulling and pushing didn't seem to do any good either.

"Monroe. Monroe!"

He blew out of the house and ran toward the car. His shoes skidded on the gravel, which was too bad because there were still a few big puddles left from the storm. Poor Monroe did a slip-and-slide into a big one. A sheet of mud went up and down his pants and past the neck of his new shirt, splattering his hair and face.

"Monroe, are you looking for Sue Jan or trying to mud wrestle?" I joked, still trapped in the convertible, a fun-fake smile on my face.

"She's gone." He scampered up and slipped back down again in the slick, wet mud.

"What do you mean she's gone?" I started rocking

my body forward and back and to the side to maneuver my way to the driver's side door.

Monroe finally succeeded in standing and swiped the back of his hand across the mud that covered the side of his face, leaving a light layer of brown. He walked over to the driver's side and opened the door just as I made it there. I stepped out.

"I looked all over the house." Concern etched all over his face, at least the parts that weren't covered in mud, he shifted from foot to foot. "I even went into the bomb shelter. She's not home."

I squinted my eyes, still doubtful. "Fallout, not bomb, shelter. Let's go inside. You may not know all the nooks and crannies in that old house the way I do."

He followed me like a sad little mud-caked puppy. "I'm not being mean or anything, but you have to agree with me on this. Sue Jan would be a hard person not to spot, like hiding a giraffe in a Volkswagen."

He gave me a weak nod. I touched his shoulder then recoiled. *Yuck, mud.* But since my hand was already muddy, I continued patting his shoulder to comfort the worried look off his face. "Let's just take another look, okay?" His face was still one big ball of worry.

In truth, Monroe and I left no stone unturned, as they say. Every closet door was opened. We looked under the beds, in the attic crawl space, in the backyard storage shed, and then suddenly remembered her car. I looked out back where she usually parked, and it was gone.

"No wonder she's not here," Monroe concluded. "She took off somewhere in her car. Call her, Lovita."

I did, but this time we were inside the house, and I heard a faint noise. I couldn't quite put my finger on where it was coming from, so I kept calling her number. Monroe followed me like a shadow from room to room. But in the kitchen we noticed that the sound seemed loudest. We looked through drawers, under the kitchen table, on the porch right outside. Then I opened the fridge and there it was—Sue Jan's powder pink cell phone covered in the bling of champagne-colored rhinestones. The phone teetered on top of a head of iceberg lettuce.

"Monroe," I said in response to this new discovery, "I'm calling Hans. He might know something about what happened."

He plucked his keys up off the kitchen counter and sprinted to the door. "Call him on the way to his house. Let's just go."

I put Sue Jan's phone down. "Okay. I'm with you. But you can't go like that. You're slimed from head to toe. Hold on."

I started to scurry away, then I spun around and gestured. "Ah, you might wanna clean up a bit while I scrounge around for something you can put on."

First through Sue Jan's, then my bedroom, I slammed dresser drawers open and shut. Nothing we owned would have fit Monroe; he was much smaller than either of us. And our clothes were too girlie. Mama had donated all of Daddy's clothes long ago. But a hasty rummage through the locker in the fallout shelter produced an unexpected surprise—something that belonged to my daddy when he was young.

Though I wasn't sure Monroe was desperate enough to wear it.

"Here you go." I heard the shower shut off. He poked his head out the door. Face freshly scrubbed and pink, he was, in fact, desperate enough to wear what I handed him.

I talked to Monroe on the other side of the bathroom door. "Hope it fits you. You're just lucky I was able to find something around this place. It was in one of the shelter lockers behind a big jar full of matchbooks."

He popped out of the bathroom. "Ready?"

Before I could answer, he was halfway to the car.

***

We pulled up in front of Hans's one-story, wood-frame house and started walking down a narrow convoluted path. Gardens surrounded the home, and literally every inch of space was occupied by a useful plant. Instead of using produce suppliers, Loo grew most of her own for the restaurant. Standing like sentinels and spaced evenly throughout the garden were bamboo teepees and trellises encased with vines. Unusual vegetables like Asian squash and slender purple eggplant hung like Christmas tree ornaments from them. I wondered where my favorite vegetable, tiny little corns, grew.

The squeaky steps to the porch worked better than any doorbell. Before we reached the top step, the porch light went on and the front door creaked open about six inches. "Who's there?" demanded Loo in a gruff voice.

I cleared my throat and managed a sappy, sweet

voice. "Loo, it's Lovita and Monroe. We're here to speak to Hans. We have to ask him some questions."

"Oh, Lovita and who?" she asked, her voice louder and not quite as gruff.

"Monroe," I answered.

"This not a good time to see Hans. He is not well. It was something he ate."

Monroe and I looked at each other. *Sue Jan's cooking.*

"Loo," I insisted, "we understand about Hans's feeling under the weather and all, but we really have to speak with him. It's about Sue Jan. She's missing and we wondered if Hans knows where she might have gone off to."

Instead of opening the door wider, Loo slithered out the crack and closed the door behind her. She stood before us in a silken dressing gown, pale aqua and pink with an overlay of embroidered florals. Her long hair hung loose almost to her waist, wherever that was. One look at her face proved the hair-pulled-back-from-the-face-in-a-tight-bun theory was correct. Loo looked like a shar-pei pup, all wrinkled and droopy.

Loo managed a short smile and looked us over, though her gaze lingered a moment on Monroe. "I am certain that my son would not know the whereabouts of MizSueJan." Her face was blank of emotion. She extended one arm curtly. "Why don't you ask him tomorrow instead? As I told you, he is not feeling well."

"Mutter? Mutter?" Hans whined from the back of the house. "Where are you?"

At last, emotion rippled across her face. "In a

moment, Hans!" she called to him. Clomping sounds came from the back of the house toward the front room, then stumbling. Loo threw open the door to reveal Hans leaning hard on a buffet table. She ran to his side. Monroe and I followed.

His face was as white as the towel wrapped around his neck, and he was shirtless. I guessed that Hans was suffering from a case of food poisoning. Maybe Sue Jan left the chicken out a little too long or something. I wasn't worried about Sue Jan though, other than the fact that she was missing. She rarely ever got sick off food. Had a stomach made of cast iron.

Loo clucked and cooed at her son as she led him to a chair. Monroe held up Hans on the opposite side. If only Suey could see him now.

The house was filled with all things exotic. Far East furniture—tables and chairs, chests, a desk, and an ornate sofa—filled the room. A thick, expensive-looking Oriental carpet covered most of the wooden floor underneath the sofa and coffee table. Carved bookcases stacked with bound books and little jade figurines lined one entire wall. Orchids tucked in all spaces between bloomed with delicious abandon. Purple and fuchsia, buttery yellow, red, and even orange, they sprinkled the room with color and gave it life. How could they afford all this stuff, running a rinky-dink restaurant in a little blink of a town?

Loo frowned at us and turned to Hans. "My son, I tell them you are sick and to go away. Maybe see you tomorrow instead."

I still couldn't get over those shar-pei wrinkles, and

when she frowned, her face looked even worse, like an old shar-pei. I guess the only thing worse than looking like a shar-pei puppy is looking like an old shar-pei dog.

Green at the gills, he waved her away a moment before regaining almost perfect posture, which I had to give him credit for doing. Talk about a mule kicking you in the stomach. I suddenly remembered Sue Jan's words. Maybe she was sick, too. Somewhere out there, sick and all alone. In the dark. Probably crying.

This time I meant business and asked him flat out. "Hans, when's the last time you saw Sue Jan?"

He coughed, and for a moment I thought he was going to be sick again. "We said good-bye at her front door."

"That's it?" Monroe almost screamed. "Was she upset about something?"

Hans looked at Monroe kinda funny for a second then doubled over in pain again. "Yesssss." He grimaced. "She was upset when I told her about m–my. . .betrothal."

Arms folded, I came up closer to him. "So you're engaged, eh? You might have mentioned that to her before accepting the dinner invite."

Hans dry heaved before the last word left my lips, then he panted. I almost felt sorry for the man, but continued nonetheless. "And tell me, did she leave? Run out of the house and jump in her car?"

"Noooo," he managed to eke out. "Sheeee ordered me to leave and slammed the door shut behind me. *After* squirting soy sauce on my shirt."

I unfolded my arms. "The fancy silk dragon shirt?

You mean she squirted soy sauce all over that?"

He forced one last nod in pain, then hand over mouth and fast as a slingshot, he ran out of the room.

Loo followed him, but then she turned to give us a disapproving look, shar-pei style.

We shut the door behind us, doubling over in laughter before reaching the car. Monroe hopped in after me.

"That Sue Jan." Monroe laughed. "What a spitfire!"

He started the engine. Our laughs tapered off.

"And she's still missing," he said.

I took his hand. "Monroe, let's pray. We're Christians, aren't we? Why didn't we pray in the first place?

"Father, please show us where Sue Jan is and how to help her. We pray that she's not sick or hurt or in any type of trouble. Lead us to her, O Lord, in Jesus' na—"

That's when newbie believer Monroe joined in with a prayer of his own. "Jesus, Lord, I thank You for Sue Jan. I love her and want what's best for her. Most of all I want her to be all right." He opened his eyes. "In Jesus' name. Amen."

By that time, my eyes were filled with tears. I remembered the fortune in Monroe's cookie that day in Chun's. If only Sue Jan could see how special Monroe Madsen really was. She had no idea that true love was *truly* only a heartbeat away.

16

Only Hunan

The drive back was quiet. As we passed down Main Street, I couldn't help but look at the shop, even in its present state. Then something caught my attention. A light, faint as a glowworm.

"Monroe, slow down. I think I see a light in the shop."

He screeched the car to a halt, slammed it into PARK, and jumped out. As I said before, he was a bit high strung about Sue Jan's disappearance. This time I shadowed *him* as he crunched over remnants of glass the cleanup crew had missed. The boutique shop door was slightly ajar, a flickering glow emanated from the beauty shop, and we were drawn to it like moths to a flame.

Sue Jan sat sprawled out in the chair at her beauty station. Two empty cartons of ice cream—double fudge and mocha marshmallow butter crunch, her favorites—flanked her on both sides. Her big mirror reflected her image, which glowed from the row of perfumed decorative candles that arrayed her station's counter. Ice cream rivulets ran down the sides of her mouth, like an ice cream vampire, and she had a glazed look in her eyes that was kind of scary.

Monroe knelt down in front of her. "Sue Jan, are

you okay? Sue Jan? Sue Jan?"

"Sue Jan." I shook her.

She started swatting the air. "Stop, stop," she whimpered. "Just leave me alone." Sue Jan had been bitten by the sugar monster for sure. In all the years I'd known my friend, this was positively the worst state I had ever seen her in.

"Monroe, would you mind going to the fridge and getting a bottle of water out for Sue Jan? We need to dilute all that ice cream in her system. Right now I think she has more ice cream than blood in her body."

Happy to help out and eager to do something positive for Sue Jan, he leaped up.

Tracks of dried tears clawed down Sue Jan's cheeks, and new ones began to drizzle. "Oh, Ita," she cried. "Hans Han doesn't even like me. He's getting married to that *Soon* gal real soon. It's an arranged marriage, but he says he loves her. And I know he meant it 'cause I saw it on his face. I've never seen Hans like that before. I went to all that trouble to cook for him, too."

"And steal his recipe," I added, going for a laugh. Sue Jan didn't take the hook though.

Short sniffles and cry hiccoughs took turns escaping her mouth. Poor Suey. She was a sight.

"Sue Jan, if it's any consolation, your dinner made Hans sick as a dog. We went over to his house, looking for you, and he was green around the gills—driving the porcelain bus when we left. He was driving the porcelain bus when we left." I had to add another thought. "And I find it difficult if not impossible to imagine Hans Han in love with anyone besides himself."

A slight smile trembled her lips. "H–he said he d–doesn't like o–overweight women. They're n–not his t–type."

Mascara pooled in deep circles under her eyes, and her nose was red from all the crying she'd been doing.

I gave her a long hug. "What does he know? I told you that Hans didn't deserve a woman like you. You're filet mignon and he's a skirt steak. You're champagne and he's vinegar. You're—"

"You're perfect," interrupted Monroe. He stood before her, holding a cold bottle of water, impeccably dressed, a handsome sight. His face bore a perfect reflection of his heart—the face of a man totally in love. For perhaps the first time, Sue Jan looked at him and understood the deepness of his unconditional love and acceptance. Raccoon-eyed, hair sticking straight up like a fright wig, and ice cream stains all down the front of her clothes, she wasn't exactly a Barbie to his Ken but, in Monroe's eyes, Sue Jan was a princess. She smiled at him. A soft, feminine, vulnerable smile—not the calculating, manipulative smiles she had thrown his way before.

He opened the cap on the bottle of water and handed it to her, then he knelt down for the second time in one night. Was he—nah—could he—was he actually going to propose?

Monroe gently took her hand in his. Some time ago I had stopped swallowing and, I believe, breathing as well, and I was starting to feel the effects. But fainting at this point was not an option. There was no way I was gonna miss this.

"Sue Jan," he started, "you know how I feel about you."

She tried to nod her head, but it fell forward loosely. I think Sue Jan had stopped breathing long before I did.

"I have the greatest respect for you and because of that, as well as what happened to my life in church this past Sunday, I have to confess something to you." He paused. "It's been bothering me."

Sue Jan sat up, her interest aroused, and noticed her reflection in the mirror. She lifted a piece of her sleeve to clean the ice cream rivulets off the corners of her mouth from her pity party à la mode. "What is it, Monroe?"

"You may have noticed that Lovita and I have been spending an awful lot of time together, and I just want you to know—"

"Monroe," I interrupted. "Is there any more water in that fridge?" I had to keep him from making the confession I knew was coming. Sue Jan was gonna have a fit.

One look from Sue Jan silenced me. She knew my ways. "What do you want me to know, Monroe? That you and Lovita are in love, too? That's all I need to hear right now." She turned her head to the side, resting her nose on a knuckle to catch the tears.

A tear glimmered in the corner of one of Monroe's eyes. "Lovita and I were just trying to make you jealous. We had a plan to pretend we liked each other so you would notice me."

Sue Jan folded her arms across her chest. I was

still behind her so all I saw was her reflection, which is, I knew, the best way to view the Medusa without getting turned to stone. However, the look Sue Jan was shooting me in the mirror was just as powerful as the Medusa's. I couldn't move an inch if I wanted to.

"So the two of you had a little plan? A little lying plan to trick me into getting green-eyed jealous over *you*? Of all the nerve."

Monroe stood and backed up a few steps. His survival instincts kicking in.

She went on. "Who do you think I am—some superficial woman who would steal a man from her best friend just to satisfy her own insecurity?"

Monroe and I looked at each other and shrugged our shoulders in affirmation.

"Never mind that." She kicked the air with her bare feet and scowled at me. "How could you, my ex-best friend, lie to me that way? Were you even listening to Pastor Meeks today? I trusted you."

"Sue Jan," I said in answer to her accusation, "I am your best friend, and I love you, and I told you that dating Hans was gonna be a huge mistake, didn't I? And didn't I also tell you that I thought Monroe was just perfect for you? That's all I was trying to do— play a little matchmaker for my best friend and my new friend, Monroe, 'cause I think the two of you are pretty special, and together you would make a pretty special couple. That's all."

"Well, that's just it. I have had it with people disappointing me, especially my friends." Sue Jan stood up and wobbled. When Monroe reached out for her, she hissed at him. "Don't you touch me." She looked my way, too. "You neither."

She pawed at the beauty station for her keys and scooped them up. "I'll be quitting my job as soon as I find another. I'll be moving out of your house as soon as I can find new accommodations. And," she added with a dash of spite, "I no longer consider the two of you as my friends."

A triumphant *harrumph* punctuated her dramatic display as she crunched out of the shop and slammed the door even though it was half off its hinges already. The open bottle of water on her beauty station tipped over and spilled. I expected to hear her car burn rubber down the street.

It was sugar tyranny. That's all it was. Poor Monroe looked like he was gonna cry. Sue Jan would be sorry for what she said the next day, but too proud to take it back. It would be months before she would own up to the wrongness of her diva display. Of course, what we did was wrong, but it felt right at the time.

Suddenly, the door burst open and Sue Jan, wild eyed and messy mopped, thrust her head in. "I just wanna know one thing before I walk out of your lives forever and ever," she said, keys jangling in her hand. "Why is Monroe dressed like Elvis?"

17

DIM SUM TIMES

Vicki-Lou woke me up with a sandpaper swish of her tongue on my cheek. I heard a low hum coming from somewhere. A squint at the bedside clock revealed the time, 7:55 a.m., but the alarm hadn't gone off. Then I realized the sound was Vicki-Lou's purring.

Her paws dug into my collarbone, and her buff and cream face stared straight at me. "Mee-ow. . .mee-ow." Her word for hungry made me an offer I couldn't refuse. The only way to get her paws off me was to get up and feed her and the other kitties. I knew from experience that the other three were waiting at the foot of my bed in case the first attempt to wake me was unsuccessful. No need to call the rest of the troops in until needed. Kitty-Mingus, Hotdog, Sunshine, and Vickie-Lou were wise in the ways of humans.

Just as I threw the sheets off, the phone started ringing. I managed a groggy hello while shuffling off to the kitchen, holding the phone between ear and shoulder while slipping one arm into my robe. I was just switching the phone to my other ear and shoulder when I heard his voice.

"Lovita?"

It was Hudson. I covered the phone with one hand

and cleared my throat so my next words would sound sweet as honey. "Hudson, is that *you*?"

"Yes, yes it is." He laughed. "Did I wake you? I know it's kind of early."

"Oh, no Hudson—Sue Jan's cats beat you to it this morning."

His voice was so deep and masculine. I couldn't catch my breath right when he spoke. And on top of that, my heart beat funny, my stomach swished around like a washing machine, and I broke out into a cold sweat.

As if holding his breath or hyperventilating, *or both*, he struggled. "I was wondering—umm, Lovita, if you would like to—umm, go out for dinner with me sometime."

Would I? How could he be nervous? I was supposed to be the nervous one.

Maintaining my composure, I somehow eased out the words with grace. "I'd like that very much."

Sunshine and Hotdog rubbed against both my legs in a simultaneous effort to get my attention, while Kitty-Mingus and Vicki-Lou meowed loudly by their empty dishes.

"Oh good," he sighed, "I mean. . ."

How could this incredibly good-looking guy be nervous about asking a woman like me out? I could understand it better if I looked like a size-double-zero supermodel instead of the fat lady at the opera people talk about. They say you can never be too thin or too rich—and I was definitely neither, so why was he interested?

"When?" I asked, in a calm voice that was nothing like I felt inside. Sunshine and Hotdog rose up on their hind legs to paw the edge of my robe. I popped the lid on a huge container of cat food and measured out four large scoops, one for each dish, then I filled a pitcher with water for their corresponding water dishes. "That should hold 'em for a while," I said, speaking my thoughts out loud.

"Huh?" He seemed confused.

Horrified, I threw the conversation into reverse. "*When* do you want to go out?"

Hudson was a dream too good to be true. Like an answer to prayer that I—

Then I remembered the prayer on the porch. Would God answer my prayer so soon and in such a perfect way?

"Oh, that's right." He laughed. "Well, I guess this coming Friday, if that's okay with you. I sure enjoyed having ice cream with you after church on Sunday. You're really a lot of fun, you know."

I was a lot of fun? A miracle unfolded before my eyes. *Call the news crews! Send out press releases. A hot-looking, godly man thinks Lovita Mae Horton is fun.*

My other slipper having fallen off somewhere, I hopped through the house on one slipper, looking for Sue Jan. Technically, she hated my guts and wasn't speaking to me, but I was sure she would make an exception in this case.

"Friday sounds good. What time?" I asked, throwing open the door to Sue Jan's bedroom. She wasn't there, though the bed was made, which was unusual for Sue

Jan. She wasn't in the bathroom either.

"Umm, how about seven o'clock?" he asked.

I almost skated through the kitchen door and onto the porch in my haste to find her. She was sitting in the same wicker chair I had been sitting in a couple of days ago. When she saw me, I noticed that she covered something on her lap with part of her robe.

"Seven sounds great," I answered enthusiastically.

"Well then—I'll look forward to seeing you," he replied in that smooth, buttery. . .completely dreamy voice.

Somehow an equally smooth reply came out of my mouth. "Until then. . ." I clicked off and found myself blowing a kiss to the phone.

"Sue Jan, did you hear that?" I screamed, jumping up and down.

A smile eclipsed her face when she realized that I had just blown a kiss to the phone.

"Hudson, right? That's nice, Lovita. I'm truly happy for you." She picked up a magazine and casually took a sip of coffee.

"That's it? That's all you have to say?" I couldn't believe it. For years I hadn't shown the slightest interest in anyone and hardly ever in front of Sue Jan, for fear of her telling the world and embarrassing me. And now—now that there really was or could be someone special and perfect and wonderful—she wasn't even a tiny bit interested.

"You're still mad, aren't you?"

She looked up from the magazine. "Mad? I was last night. Furious, in fact." She flipped a page and looked back down at it. "Today I just feel disappointed in you, Lovita, and in Monroe. And in my life right now."

Sue Jan stood up. "Now, if you'll excuse me, I don't feel like discussing this anymore."

"You don't feel like what?" I asked defiantly. "First off, Monroe and I did what we did because we both care about you, although I have to wonder why. Second, you're just mad because you're the one who does this sort of thing. You're always doing something crazy, and I'm usually the last to know about it. For once, just once, I did something out of the ordinary, and it was for a good cause. It was for you. And you're mad about it."

Sue Jan gave me one last condescending look and disappeared into the house.

My thoughts were so mixed up and troubled. There was just no making sense of things. Frustrated, I sank into my favorite wicker chair and reached for my Bible on the table next to it. But it was gone. I looked behind the plant, where I usually kept it. Not there either. *Maybe it fell.*

I looked under the table, even under my chair cushion, and still, no Bible. Part of me wondered if she knew where it was. I'd even caught her a few times before, using it as a makeshift lap table to do her nails on. Sacrilege! But because of the mood she was in, I didn't even want to go near Sue Jan, much less confront her.

A muted knock sounded against the solid oak front door. On the way to answer it, I spotted my other slipper under the kitchen table and put it back on.

I swung the front door wide open. Monroe stood

outside dressed in one of his new casual outfits, a blue polo shirt and tan pants. I had to do a double take at first. Seemed like every time I saw Monroe, he looked thinner and better.

"Hey, Monroe, come on in." I made a point of looking him over. "Nice threads, but that wasn't one we bought, was it?"

Monroe flushed crimson as soon as I mentioned it. "Well, not exactly. You see—I went back to that store and bought a few more things."

I beamed with pride. "That's good, Monroe. You did a great job, picking this outfit. It goes together well and it fits you. By the way, are you losing some weight?"

He pressed his lips together, his face flushed pink. "I guess I haven't been eating that much in between meals."

"Well, you look good. Better than I do. I'm still in my robe and look a sight. Hudson called this morning and asked me out on a real date. What do you think of that?"

Monroe seemed uncomfortable to be thrust in the position of girlfriend. But I was desperate to tell someone my good news.

After I stopped in the kitchen to grab a pitcher of raspberry tea and some glasses, he followed me onto the porch, where he sank into a squeaky wicker chair, but thankfully not my favorite one. In an attempt to find a comfortable position, he squeaked to the right, then creaked to the left, then just gave up and sat straight forward, hands on the arm rests. "That sounds good to me. Hudson seems like a good guy. You two would make a nice couple."

"Why Monroe." I couldn't help smiling. "What a sweet thing to say."

Sue Jan strolled onto the porch as if she had forgotten something, though I knew full well that *she* knew full well that Monroe Madsen was sitting right there on the porch in the rickety-crickety old wicker chair she'd bought at a garage sale for fifty cents.

A surprised look on her face set the stage. "Lov— oh, I'm sorry, did I interrupt you two making some plots or plans? I forgot that magazine I was reading. Is it over here?" She bent over and started rooting through a pile of magazines on the table. "Did you happen to see it?" she added, trying to sound bland and emotionless.

Monroe stared, enraptured at her presence. Swathed in a diaphanous freesia-hued dress with a silky sheath underneath, she'd done a quick change. A whiff of fragrant blossoms hung in the air wherever she moved. Probably that new shower spray she bought from a catalogue last month. Smelled good, though. I looked at Monroe—thoroughly dazzled by her splendor.

"No, I haven't seen your magazine," I answered in the same vanilla way. Then I got fired up and couldn't help myself. "I was sure you took it with you, but while we're on the subject, have you seen my Bible? It's gone missing. You're not using it to do your nails again, are you? 'Cause if you are, that's pure blasphemy, and I'll sic Hazel and Inez on you for sure."

Sue Jan stood up straight and brushed some stray

strands of upswept hair from her face. "Why Lovita, I'm sure I don't know what you're talking about. Your Bible is right there on top of the table."

My jaw fell open in amazement. There it was, plain as day, right in the middle of the table, next to the jade plant. "But it. . ." I pointed. "The—the Bible wasn't. . ." The words kept stopping.

Sue Jan uttered a *hmmph* and strode with purposeful steps down the porch out to her car. I affectionately called it her "clown car," a foreign automobile, micro sporty, and useless in every way except for show. Sue Jan could scarcely breathe in it, much less drive the thing or afford it, but as soon as she saw it, she had to have it. Oh, and of course it was red, "the color of passion." Because above all else, Sue Jan was passionate about everything.

"Where are you going?" Monroe followed her.

She pushed past him with a swish of her hand. "To do some errands." Sue Jan squeezed into the front seat of her circus car, now somewhere between sizzling and searing hot. "Oouch, ouch, ikes—that's hot!" she screeched.

He smiled, I guessed hoping she would notice. "Want some company?"

She sucked in her cheeks. "Nooo," she uttered, enunciating through pink glossed lips. "I don't think so." With that, Sue Jan shut the car door, revved the engine, and took off with a wave.

Forlorn and forsaken, Monroe stood right where her car had left him, his hand still in the air. After her car was just a dot in the distance, I called him back onto the porch.

"How about some lunch and a little detective work?" I asked, pouring tall glasses of raspberry tea. "I'll make us some turkey-and-bacon club sandwiches. And we'll have some chips and sliced watermelon on the side."

A smile bobbed up and surfaced for a moment on his face. "I'd like that."

18

FIVE-SPICE VICE

Pad in hand after lunch, I leaned back in my favorite porch chair, pencil poised. "Monroe, there's got to be some sort of sense to the fortunes. Otherwise, why would whoever sent them even bother? There are much easier ways to get in touch with people. Why send a smoke signal when you can just pick up a cell phone?"

"Maybe they're afraid."

I started scribbling fortune cookie shapes and doodling faces on the page. "I think that whoever sent the clues in the fortune cookies wants to tell us something, but he—or she—wasn't exactly truthful about the man in the hat telling me more. Clint didn't know any more than I did. It was obviously just a way to get Clint and I to join forces and investigate. But why? And who?"

I looked over at him, watching as he brushed his hands over his head then clasped them behind his neck for an instant pillow. " 'True love is only a heartbeat away,' " he repeated in a soft, daydreamy voice. Looking up at the porch ceiling, he kept repeating it. Monroe obviously had something else on his mind.

"Monroe, snap out of it! I need some help."

He bolted upright. "O–okay. Sorry."

"Clint told me he was taking a quick trip to New Mexico."

"Really? Why do suppose he's going there?"

I snapped my fingers. "I wonder. . ."

"What?"

"At Sammich's the other day, there was a report on TV about some top secret information stolen from Los Alamos in New Mexico. Clint was real interested. He zipped out the door faster than a greased leopard."

Monroe gulped. "You mean the national laboratory?"

I snapped my fingers again. "Yup, that's it."

"That's serious." He stood up and thrust both hands in his pockets, jangling the coins in them as he paced. "Lovita, you may be mixed up in something big—dangerous, too. Maybe you should let the police handle this."

I strummed on the table next to me. "They haven't done a thing yet. I realize this isn't a high priority to them—a cold case I guess. They're still straightening things out from the storm."

I went into the kitchen and returned with a fresh pitcher of raspberry tea and two slices of lemon meringue pie. I sat, elbows on the table, and clasped my hands together. "Monroe, with Clint out of town, it's up to us. If there's anything to this funny fortune, we've got to investigate on our own."

His brow creased. "I don't know about that, Lovita. Why can't Clint or the Bentley police handle this?"

"The Bentley police? I'll tell you why. They never even returned my calls. I asked Clint to check it out for me but I haven't heard back from him yet."

"Oh. But don't you think it's funny the sheriff hasn't called you back? They're pretty much on the ball in that town from what I hear. And lawyers hear a lot, believe me. I even heard more about Jolene's son since our visit to the beauty supply shop. If I was a public defender, I'd be seeing a lot of him."

I had to smile. "Monroe, you really are a hoot. Sue Jan's a blessed woman to have you."

He rubbed his eye with the palm of his hand. "Do me a favor, Lovita, and tell her that. Will you?"

I took a bite of pie. "Well, if the Bentley police are so on the ball, as you seem to think, why haven't they returned my calls or come by to investigate? There has to be a reason. Ummm." All the while, the gears I imagined were in my head clicked and clanked.

I heard something and got up to look out the window. A truck zoomed right up to the house, leaving a trail of dust in its wake. A young man in a brown uniform left the engine running, hopped out, and rang the doorbell five or six times before I could get to the front door. Just as I opened it, I saw him salute a hello from inside his truck, kick it in REVERSE, switch it into DRIVE, and then floor it down the road.

"What is it?" asked Monroe.

I picked up the feather light box from the doormat. It didn't seem worth all the effort to have a box this small delivered. We sat down on the front porch swing while I opened it, and we both caught our breath at the sight of the lone item inside.

A fortune cookie.

"Open it," urged Monroe. "Whoever sent the other fortunes had to be the one who sent this one, too!"

My fingers felt numb. I couldn't seem to grip the

wrapper right to open it, so Monroe pulled the cookie from my hand and smashed it like Sue Jan would. He tore open the cellophane wrapper and picked out the fortune. Then, gentleman that he was, Monroe handed it straight to me.

> *I have your friend. She will meet the same fate as your father unless you meet me at the Cut 'n Strut tonight at 6:00. Do not contact the authorities.*

I gasped. "Sue Jan!"

Monroe reached for the paper, read it, and immediately called her cell phone. While he tried to reach her, I looked in the fridge to see if history had repeated itself, though I was certain I would have seen it when I'd cut the pie earlier. It wasn't there.

The world seemed to be caving in all around me. Suddenly I could contain it no longer and began to sob. All the emotions I'd been letting out in dribs and drabs, since opening that first fortune cookie, flooded out. My knees weak, I sank down. Lying down on the cool tile of the kitchen floor seemed to help. Monroe, hearing my sobs, ran in.

He pulled me off the floor. "Are you okay?"

I managed a nod between an earthquake of stuttering cries that I was unable to stop. He tried to lift me to my feet, but I shook my head.

"We need to call the police. She doesn't answer her phone. Gotta go look for her." He reached for his keys.

"N–no." I shook my head. "The message said not to call the authorities. Remember?"

He paced back and forth. "Right." Then he paced himself right into the living room, where I heard him mumbling.

"Monroe, we have to wait until 6:00. W—what are you doing?"

"I know. . . ," his voice echoed back. "I'm praying."

Still weak in the knees and feeling faint, I lay down, my right cheek against the kitchen floor, and couldn't help noticing that it was in desperate need of a good sweep. There were crumbs everywhere and little bits of celery and ringlets of green onion. That's when I noticed an oblong piece of paper on the floor, covered by the cabinet overhang. I rocked my body, swishing fishlike across the floor, till I reached it. Hans's recipe for kung pao chicken. *Funny, some of the quantities for ingredients were in purple ink. Why didn't I notice that before? Would Hans Han have kidnapped Sue Jan just to get his stupid recipe back?*

I sat up and held the recipe over my head and had a sudden flash of recognition. The purple ink on the fortune. . .purple ink on the recipe. Could it be? No, too far-fetched an idea. No way.

"Monroe."

"Yes?"

"Would you mind bringing me the fortune from my purse in the living room?"

Either someone was in love with purple ink, or there was more than kung pao chicken cooking in the kitchens at Chun's and Cheng's!

Egg Drop Toupee

At the kitchen table, pad and pencil before me again, I wrote down the numeral quantity for every ingredient from Hans's recipe for kung pao chicken. As it turned out, there was a lot of numbers. Too many for a lucky number on a fortune cookie fortune. But the ones in purple were just right. Twelve.

I wrote down all the purple ones and had Monroe read off the lucky numbers on the fortune.

"Ready, Lovita?"

"Fire when ready."

"Okay then: 4—1—2—1—2—1—4—2—2—1—2—1." Silent at first, he asked me to read them off to him this time.

"All right: 4—1—2—1—2—1—4—2—2—1—2—1."

I pushed the recipe closer to Monroe, and he pushed the fortune right next to it. Our eyes met.

"Perfect," I whispered. "It shouldn't. . . . Could it be a coincidence?"

"Too perfect." Monroe pushed his chair back and walked away from the table, rubbing the back of his neck. "A spy ring right under our noses here in Wachita, the friendliest town in the US-of-A."

I grabbed the phone.

"What are you doing?"

"Putting a call in to Clint."

"But the message said—"

"I know what it said, but this is bigger than you and I can handle."

Monroe grabbed my hand. "What if they hurt Sue Jan?"

I laid my hand over his. "Monroe, we'll pray for her, but believe me, Sue Jan Pritchard would want us to blow the whistle on a ring of spies serving up secrets and Szechwan."

He let his hand fall. "You're right." He leaned against the wall and gave one quick nod.

After two rings, the call went directly to Clint's message box. "Awrgh!" I let the phone slip from my hand to the table and rested my face in my palms.

Monroe spread out his hands, palms down, on the table and stared at them. I could tell he was worried. "You should leave a message."

I took his advice and called again. This time when I heard the electronic away message, I left my own. I detailed everything we knew about the recipe, the fortune, and the upcoming rendezvous.

Speaking of that, while waiting for the rendezvous, magic hour, Monroe and I searched through the house for any clues as to where Sue Jan might have gone. Funny, these days we seemed to be forever searching the house because of Sue Jan.

We didn't find any other interesting papers, except some love letters she had written to Hans Han but never sent, and I'm the one that found those. I didn't have the heart to show Monroe the notebook page with *Mrs. Hans Han* written in various ways all over it, with hearts adorning each signature. She drew stick figure pictures, too, and one of 'em was of a girl with a veil on her little round head, holding a bouquet. I never realized how much Sue Jan was pinning her hopes on a solid relationship with Hans. Some friend I was—Sue Jan's emotions crushed and without a shoulder to cry on.

And now my best friend in the whole wide world was missing—kidnapped by someone for some unknown reason. The tears wouldn't stop flowing. I grew more anxious with every passing second.

After I fed the cats, who were circling like sharks and meowing for supper, we sat down with some freshly brewed coffee to brainstorm again.

I touched my fingertips together and tapped them in the rhythm of my thoughts. "What if there's some kind of code in the numbers we could crack? You know—like the kind we'd decipher with those secret decoders we used to get in cereal boxes and such. The numbers tell you which words are. . ." I stopped suddenly, remembering my secret decoder ring. It wasn't on my pinkie. I'd taken it off my finger before showering.

A quick dash to bathroom, and I saw I'd left it on the counter by my toothbrush. As I turned to rush out, I couldn't help but notice my brand-new shower curtain, given the dalmatian treatment with blotches of black mascara. Sue Jan's crying jag the night before had left its mark. *Poor Sue Jan.* Seeing those spots on my brand-new shower curtain made me more determined than ever to rescue my friend.

I returned and showed the ring to Monroe. The idea registered on his face. Taken by the thought of it, he added, "Yesss, like when we were kids. I used to have a secret decoder ring and I—"

"Of course, it's just a hunch, but why not try it? That's what I say. Anything to help us find Sue Jan faster—before anything happens, God forbid. I feel so helpless."

I spoke the fear that was swimming around in my head, then I felt like dirt when Monroe's face fell. He could go from enthusiasm to depression in zero point two seconds. I touched his hand. "Let's just get to this. We might find something to help us rescue Sue Jan. And catch whoever murdered my father."

Monroe manned the decoder ring, and I held the pencil to paper. We tried number to number, number to letter, first and third letters, even and odd numbers. All the simple codes we could find or think of. Together we tried every combination in our heads and on the ancient decoder ring. But nothing made any sense.

At least the time ticked away faster. Before we knew it, the hands on the kitty clock were at 4:30, then 5:00. Without saying a word, we both got up and headed toward the door. Monroe went out to start the car. But before I left, I picked up the recipe and my fortune and sealed them in an envelope. I wrote *Clint Greech* across it in big red letters and slipped it into my purse.

THE WAY THE
COOKIE CRUMBLES

We passed Cheng's and I scowled. Though I longed to have a knock-down-drag-out with Dragon Lady Loo, not to mention Hans, Monroe and I had more pressing matters to attend to. We pulled up in front of Lovita's Cut 'n Strut, or rather what was left of it, round about 5:15 p.m., plenty of time before 6:00. Blue tarp covered where the glass in the picture window should have been. The sign was gone—splintered, picked up, and swept up. I got out of the car and approached the shop. Its glass door rested on a lone hinge. Through a small gap, I could still smell Sue Jan's vanilla-and-apricot candle from her pity party the other night. *Oh Sue Jan, I miss you.*

We decided to kill some time over a cup of coffee, so we walked down the street to the Texas Star. Callie met us at the door with a menu and a knowing look, and she took us directly to a booth I requested. The café was full, and I recognized some of the men from the khakis crowd. From the way their forks were poised in midair, I could tell they recognized us, too. We sat down. From this vantage point, Monroe and I could see right down the street. Callie plonked down two coffees and a tiny plate of creams.

Before she turned to leave us, I tugged the hem of her apron and put the envelope in it. In a low voice, I motioned her to lean in close. "Callie, if anything should happen to us, not that anything would, please see that Clint Greech gets this. He's the man—"

"With the Stetson. I've see him around town." Her nostrils flared slightly. "You got it." She stood up straight and attempted to play it cool. "Sure, the restrooms are over thataway, ma'am." She pointed with her pencil then stuck it behind her ear and walked off.

Monroe kicked my foot under the table, then he nodded his head toward the lunch counter. I looked over and saw Hudson staring right at us. *How could I have missed seeing him?* He left his burger and fries at the counter where he was sitting and walked over to the booth, looking like the wind was knocked out of him. "Hi, Lovita. Hi, Monroe." He held out his hand for a quick shake. "How are you guys doing?"

I popped out a nervous smile, wondering if my lip trembled any. I couldn't help it. How could I feel guilty about something there wasn't anything to feel guilty about? Looking up, I noticed again how good-looking Hudson was. He had a profile like a movie star's. To make matters worse, he was wearing jeans and a navy polo shirt that showed off his muscles. And I love men with muscular physiques. Mind you, not body-builder types with their deltoids, steroids, and all that, which can be too much of a good thing.

Why wasn't Hudson smiling? Here I was, ready to swoon, and all I could think about was how much

I longed to see him smile. He was too concerned and disappointed, I guessed. And somehow, some which-a-way, that made me glad. He cared that I was sitting in a booth, having lunch with another guy. Jealous? No way. No one in my entire life had ever been jealous of me. My heart did a flip. I wished I could tell him what was going on, but there wasn't time.

Hudson leaned in closer to me, face concerned. "Lovita, are—are we still on for Friday night?" he whispered. The white of his teeth peeked between his lips, flashing the hint of a gorgeous smile when he spoke. I was half mesmerized by his teeth alone before I could answer.

"Of course we are. I–I'm looking forward to it. Really." I looked over at Monroe. "We just have some stuff to do right now," I said, reassuringly. "I—I promise to tell you all about it later. Okay?" I punctuated my answer with a hopeful smile.

He nodded in relief but still wasn't a hundred percent convinced that everything was okay. Hudson must have had a natural nose for hijinks; he knew something was going on, all right.

He picked up my hand and kissed it, then he stared into my eyes. "Okay then, I'll pick you up at seven o'clock."

Then he strolled back to the lunch counter to finish his cold burger. I could easily have warmed it for him, though, what with the nuclear fusion going on in my heart. *Woowee.*

Another beneath-the-table kick from Monroe brought me back to reality. "Lovita," Monroe whispered,

"I hope he doesn't think we're together. I don't want to mess things up between the two of you."

"Don't worry about it. We'll explain later." While Monroe sipped his coffee, I downed mine fast, almost in one gulp. "C'mon, Monroe. Let's get out of here."

Once outside, we passed a few men working on one of the two intersection lights in town damaged by the storm. Some stores besides the beauty shop were still closed, but otherwise, it was business as usual.

Back in the Cut 'n Strut, we reclined in the two chairs nearest the door and waited. I crossed my legs and pumped my foot up and down. Monroe twiddled his thumbs and sighed a lot. Sure enough, at 6:00 sharp, an Asian delivery guy I recognized as Loo's waiter strolled down the street with a white paper delivery bag in hand.

Monroe and I both got up and headed toward the doorway.

I elbowed Monroe. "He's the one who spilled the tray the other night at Loo's."

Expressionless, the waiter knocked and handed me the bag. Without saying a word, he turned and walked at a brisk pace, soon disappearing down a side street.

I opened the bag and pulled out a Chinese take-out container, empty except for a lone fortune cookie in a wrapper. Monroe did the honors, smashing it as before. I plucked out the message and read.

"Follow the gray car."

"What kind of fools do they take us for?" I

scrunched the bag, frustrated.

"It could be a trap, Lovita." Monroe stared at the wall in front of him, deep in thought.

I bit into my fingernail. "But what other choice do we have?"

Monroe and I glanced at each other, then I opened the door and looked out. A gray car with dark tinted windows—the same gray rental car I'd seen twice before on the day we went shopping; once on the way to Bentley and later in Bentley itself—was parked down the street, with the engine running. Exhaust cloud puffs swirled white and toxic behind it.

Slowly, we exited the shop and strolled purposefully toward Monroe's car. An electrician engrossed in the innards of an electrical box barely noticed us as we passed.

As soon as we hopped in Monroe's car, the gray car sped off.

"Follow that car, Monroe!" I stomped on the floorboard as if I were driving.

He cast a quick glance from the wheel. "This is probably the most dangerous thing either of us has ever done."

"I know, but"—I pulled out my cell—"just in case we get in trouble, I'll call Clint again." The phone rang and rang, so I left a message with the latest details.

"I'll bet it won't be long before Clint is hot on the trail behind us." I clicked the phone shut.

"If he ever listens to his messages." Monroe was clearly worried about that.

I leaned back into the car seat, feeling a little

smug. "Don't worry. By the time he catches up with us, I hope we've already found Sue Jan and cracked this—this case or whatever it is they call it."

We followed the gray car right into Bentley, all the way through to the far end of town. We drove past the church where we thought we had seen Sue Jan's picture. I wondered if Christian ladies in all the surrounding counties were praying for her. "Well, she sure needs it now," I said out loud.

Monroe looked confused.

"Just praying," I explained. *And wondering why anyone would want to shanghai Sue Jan.*

At the edge of town, the car took a left on a narrow side street. We parked right off the main street, beside a hardware store. We got out of the car fast, though we were supposed to play it cool, like we had all the time in the world. I didn't wait for Monroe to be a gentleman and open my door. Instead I was out of the car before he was. So much for all the time in the world.

I put on a pair of sunglasses and urged Monroe to do likewise, even though it was technically nighttime. We *were* working undercover, after all. The two of us strolled down the street, even pausing to window-shop at the hardware store, of all places, like we needed a good hammer or something. Then we looked both ways, as if we would know if anybody was following us, and slipped down the side street.

A small gray car was parked out in back of a small warehouse. The overhead sign read GOLDEN TIGER IMPORTS. I thought of what Sue Jan had said. Bo told her the fortune cookies were from a place called Golden something. Could this be the place?

We skulked in silence. I'd never skulked before in my life, but we managed it. All the windows appeared to be painted over, but around the back of the warehouse we found one pane where some of the paint had come off at the bottom. And that's the one we peeked through.

There were umpteen rows of shelves filled with exotic products and boxes. And though there were banks of florescent lights, the only light on was a lone bulb hanging workshop fashion from the ceiling in the middle of the place.

A movement inside the warehouse caught our attention. Someone in a cap and bulky team jacket, though I couldn't make out which one. Had to be our driver, now walking toward the back of the warehouse. The person took a ninety-degree turn left, and we lost sight of him. We waited a few minutes, trying to figure out what to do, and then Monroe looked at me. "Lovita, you stay here. I'm going in."

I swallowed hard. Was this a new Monroe? Or just a man crazy in love?

"If you're going in, Monroe Madsen, then so am I. There's no way I'm waiting around out here by my lonesome."

He nodded, apparently realizing it would be useless to argue with me. The first thing we tried was the back door, which was locked, as expected. But to our surprise, the window we had been looking through was unlocked. We opened it and found out the hardest part about breaking and entering for us was the entering part. It was hard squeezing into the window frame and then dropping down onto the floor of the room without creating a commotion, even though I'm pretty used to squeezing into clothes and through doorways and such. I was sure I had bruises in places that had never been bruised before and won't likely ever be again.

Once we were in, Monroe shut the window—almost without a sound. I noticed that our clothes were all smudged from the dusty window and dirty floor.

We worked our way through the warehouse, recreating the driver's path to the back, and took a left at the shelves. And there it was. . .a door. . .a big metal door that kinda reminded me of Daddy's fallout shelter.

"How are we gonna get in there?" I whispered.

"I don't know, but—"

Before he was able to finish, we heard a metallic grinding sound and saw the wheel handle on the door turning. The door opened toward us, and the person in the cap and jacket stepped out of the lighted doorway, his face concealed by the darkness of the warehouse. As the door began to shut, Monroe grabbed hold of the edge and pulled it wide open. Ignited with his bravado, I charged in after him, but I stopped short, noticing cap-and-jacket's surprised face. A face I knew.

I turned and went back, though Monroe tried to stop me. The silhouette of the person, dark against the light of the open door. A quick swipe and the hat was off. "Bo?"

"Yes, MizLovita. I–I'm sorry. I had to get you here. I'll explain. . ."

"Is this some sort of trap?" Monroe pounded his fist on the stone wall of the underground cavern.

"Let's go!" She grabbed at both of us and began walking rapidly. Little lights in the walls came on as she passed. Motion detectors.

"Wait!" I heard her whisper, in the loudest whisper I'd ever heard, but we were already galloping down the dark cavern corridor after her.

At the end of the corridor were other silhouettes, of men with guns. They didn't seem surprised to see us. The men took my purse and cell and Monroe's wallet. They had the three of us bound with our hands behind our backs before we could spit. What puzzled us most, though, was when they tied Bo's hands as well. That just didn't make any sense. If she brought us to them and it was a trap, then why? And she didn't put up any kind of fight either. She wouldn't even look me in the eye. I don't know why, but I felt sorry for her even if she was a kidnapper and who knows what else.

In the ever-increasing light, I noticed some of the men were blond with blue eyes or dark-haired with blue eyes and others were Asian. Instructions were sharp and short to us, *this way* or *that way* with a foreign accent like Hans Han's. A definite connection there.

We wove down corridors carved from rock and realized we were going deeper underground. It was moist in areas, even slippery. I smelled Chinese food as we passed one section. My nose knows food. Finally, they led us into a large cavernous room. A kitchen. There were banks of stainless steel counters on all sides and a large island in the middle where an Asian man, probably in his late twenties, sat, his ankle chained to the floor. A crude hand-printing machine, strewn with fortunes, was by the wall behind him.

Clint was right about the fortunes being printed here in the US.

The chain around the kitchen prisoner's ankle was pretty long. Long enough, I guessed, for him to cook or bake and clean up at all the stations in the kitchen. The island covered in cooking pans, the man folded and shaped golden circles fresh out of the oven and stuffed each with a fortune.

Our captors led us past the man, whose eyes lit up when he saw Bo. The chains rattled when he tried to stand. A man with a gun lowered it to show he meant business, and the prisoner, though reluctant, eased back down on the stool.

We were led into a storeroom in back of the kitchen, filled with boxes and boxes of fortune cookies on shelves and on the floor. But in a dark corner, on a worn mattress, I saw a large familiar shape sitting up.

I broke free and ran forward. "Sue Jan."

"Lovita, Monroe, is that you?" she rasped.

That's when we heard the guns click. I felt someone grab my arm and push me down to the mattress next to her. Monroe wasn't so lucky. When they pushed him, he lost his balance, which is hard to keep with your hands tied behind your back. He knocked his knee on the hard floor on the way down before settling on the other side.

Before the men left, taking Bo with them, Sue Jan mustered enough strength to yell, "When are you outlaws gonna bring some food? I don't even care if you bring me some Jenny Craig meals. I'm starving back here. I haven't had a decent meal since you kidnapped me, which, by the way, is against the law. And this here man's a lawyer." She pointed to Monroe, who tried without success to quiet her. "Now you're in for it. If you were looking for trouble, now you found it. And you're gonna pay for that knee, too, or my name isn't Sue Jan Pritchard. Why, I'll bet there's a Texas-sized bruise on it by now."

I couldn't help smiling. These spies already had trouble enough. They had Sue Jan.

21

Gun Powder Tea

Sue Jan and I couldn't stop the tide of nervous giggles at first. We were just so happy to see each other. Monroe and I were just plain relieved that Sue Jan was okay. But was she? And for that matter—were we?

I looked around. No windows. No way out but the way we came in. And when the guards shut the door, I heard the key turn in the lock. A small window in the storeroom door revealed part of the back of the Asian man's head. I guess he was hard at work baking all those fortune cookies. I made a mental note to ask Sue Jan about him.

"I've already tried every way I could think of to get out of here. But there just isn't any. The door is the only way in or out. If we mean to escape, it's gonna have to be that way." Sue Jan drew in a long breath.

Then she started wiggling her hands and contorting them a strange way. She rocked her hands forward and back, then in a circular pattern. Then she bent her wrist a weird way. Soon, one hand with bubblegum pink nail polish popped out of the restraints, followed a second later by the other. Sue Jan showed us how to do it, but neither Monroe nor I could, so she helped us get out of our restraints as well.

"With all the free time on my hands," she cooed,

"I figured out how to git outta these plastic cuffs like a regular Who-dini."

"You must be double-jointed," Monroe marveled.

"I've known you all my life and I never knew," I added.

Relieved, we rubbed our wrists. Even though I was impressed with Sue Jan's newly acquired skill, I had to ask. "What happened? How'd you get yourself kidnapped and all?"

Without shower facilities, not to mention good conditioner *and makeup*, Sue Jan's mascara had done panda circles around her eyes, and her hair, usually coiffed, coddled, and cared for, was a tangled mess. "Well. . ." She drew in a breath and glanced side-a-ways at both of us. "You know how upset I was feeling the day I took off?"

I reached for her hand. "I know and I'm sorry Sue Jan. I should have been a better friend."

A look of amazement passed over her eyes, but she continued. "Well, I was really needing some comfort food, so I drove to Cheng's. I sat in a back booth because I didn't want anyone to see me or find me there. But then I looked at the menu and saw they were having a lunch special that day on kung pao chicken, of all things, and I couldn't stand it, so I called Bo on my cell phone to come and join me. I really needed someone to talk to." She paused to take a breath.

"Then what happened?" I asked.

"She joined me right away, but she wasn't herself. Bo seemed sadder than me, and preoccupied. Of course she listened to me talk, but she seemed even more interested when I talked about *your* problems and how you were trying to find out what all them clues mean and all. But then something strange happened. . . ."

Monroe couldn't contain himself any longer. "So, what happened?"

Sue Jan tore off part of her sleeve and blew her nose. "When the waiter brought the food, Bo looked nervous and kind of worried. She excused herself, said she had somewhere to go, and left her food right where it was. That made me even more depressed, and you know what I do when I'm depressed. I ate my food and started on hers, but then the room began to spin."

"And?" I wished she'd get to the point.

She sneezed. "I woke up here. What do you think? They knocked me out with kung pao. They kung pao kidnapped me."

I had to wonder why. Could Sue Jan possibly be a threat?

"They kept asking me about the recipe I borrowed from Hans. They sounded real mad at Bo for giving it to me. I overheard 'em talking about how she's a traitor and all."

"Then that's why they took her. She's a prisoner, too?"

"I think so. I honestly don't know what happened to the recipe, though. Everything's a blur. When the evening with Hans fell apart, so did I."

I looked around the room again. Cool, but not as damp as the hallways. From floor to ceiling were ten-by-twelve-sized boxes Sue Jan assured us were filled with fortune cookies. Monroe guessed there was some sort of dehumidifier hooked up to take care of the humidity in the kitchen and storeroom.

He whistled. "It's like a—a fortune cookie—factory."

Sue Jan flashed a wide grin at him. "You're exactly right, Monroe." She held out an arm and swept it over the interior. "All these boxes you see here are filled with 'em."

"How do you know?" I asked, doubtful. "I mean, all these boxes could be filled with something else and only have FORTUNE COOKIES stamped on the outside."

She shook her head forcefully. "Nope, I'm one hundred percent sure these boxes contain fortune cookies." Pointing to a nearby shelf, she said, "Monroe, see that there box, no not that one—the one next to it. That's it. Pull that one off the shelf and bring it on over here, will ya?"

Monroe handed it to her, but he shook it first. "It—it seems so light. Is there anything in it?"

She opened it and showed both of us. It was filled with wrappers, crumbs, and fortunes, but no cookies. "I got hungry last night, and they wouldn't give me anything to eat except a stale bologna sandwich on white bread, a MoonPie, and a Pepsi."

My brows arched. "So you ate an entire box of fortune cookies?"

"Sure did, Lovita, and I might do it again tonight if that's all we git to eat," she answered, defiant.

I picked up a handful of the crunchy papers and pulled them out one by one to examine them. "Hey, a few of these are different from the ones I'm used to seeing. The ink for some of the lucky numbers is purple instead of pink."

Together, the three of us went through the entire lot. Only five fortunes in the box had purple ink numbers printed on them.

"Now, why do you suppose that is?" Monroe mumbled, deep in thought.

I pondered it as well. "Maybe they just ran out of pink ink or something."

"Orrr, the purple ones are special in some way," Sue Jan said.

I marveled at her. *The CIA is sure to notice her abilities someday.*

Footsteps clacked on the hard floor of the kitchen. We scrambled to throw all the fortunes back in the box. Monroe closed it up and slid it back on the shelf just in time to work his hands back into the restraints. And there we were, three bumps on a log.

Two guards dressed in black and holding weapons entered first. Behind them, Loo strode in, calm and confident.

Her long black hair was slicked back as usual in a tight knot on the back of her head—the instant facelift look. But instead of her usual attire, she wore a casual suit and starched pinpoint shirt underneath. Open-toed medium heels in black showed off her bright red toenail polish. Loo was dressed to the nines.

In all the years I'd seen her at the restaurant, I'd never seen the Dragon Lady dressed like that. It was like a Manchurian makeover.

She brought her hands together as if happy to see us. "Hello, my friends. Of course, Sue Jan, we have already made welcome as our guest. But how nice of you to invite your friends."

Sue Jan was so mad, her cheeks flushed red. "I feel about as welcome as a hair on a biscuit." She spit out her words flavored with righteous venom.

I leveled my gaze at Loo. "Exactly why is Sue Jan your prisoner? And for that matter, why are we?"

Loo stepped forward. One of the guards pulled a metal folding chair out and set it behind her. She floated down to it in as graceful a fashion as I've ever seen. "In answer to your question, why don't you ask your friend Bo?"

"That's another thing I don't understand. Bo is a prisoner like us. How could she have kidnapped Sue Jan and tricked us into being your prisoners, too?"

Loo flashed a knowing smile. "She is the one who sent you the messages."

"Yeah, I learned how to add things up in elementary school."

"Yes." Loo hissed the *s* longer than she needed to. "We know of her treachery to us. We have an old saying, 'Seeing once is better than hearing a hundred times.'"

"What do you mean?"

Loo laughed. "She brought you something, I believe. A recipe? Hmm, and certain matters, of no small importance, were written on it. We would not have known for quite some time if my son had not been your 'special' dinner guest that night. He happened to see the recipe, in his own handwriting, protruding from a drawer in your rather quaint kitchen.

"Then how did *I* find it?" I asked.

"It is unfortunate. But after my son placed the

recipe in the pocket of his silk shirt, it must have slipped out in his haste to leave. He favors his late father in that regard. Poor attention to detail."

I couldn't stop myself; I had to keep talking and challenging her. "I knew it! Nobody has handwriting that neat unless there's something wrong with them."

She paused to purse her rouged lips. "Tell me where it is. Now!"

I looked around and decided to propose a bargain. "Set them free and I'll tell you."

Her lips turned down. "MizLovita, I assure you that you will tell us all we need to know—with or without your consent. We have ways of getting the truth from people."

The door swung open again, this time to reveal Hans Han, also dressed in a black business suit, looking sharper and suaver than ever. On one arm he sported Mafia bling—a watch all crusted over with diamonds. He sure paid attention to details when he got dressed.

He joined Loo and bent over to kiss her cheek.

"Ah, my son." She offered a wide smile. "Of course, you all know my son, Hans, don't you? But especially Sue Jan."

Hans cast a taunting glance her way, and Sue Jan covertly squeezed my hand, her bonds already undone again. Monroe sat bolt straight, as if he planned to leap off the mattress like Superman. One of the guards, apparently sensing hostility, gripped his weapon tighter and took a step forward. Monroe, helpless with his hands bound behind him, didn't budge.

"Having you here is a bit of a nuisance, one which

we shall deal with soon." Loo's voice dripped sarcasm. "I should not complain, however. You two ladies have caused me to do good business all of these years." She accented her words with a cruel laugh, joined by Hans. "Every meal is eaten like it is the last. In fact, you ate so many wontons, you now weigh one ton between you." She snickered.

I thought Sue Jan would explode. In fact, I expected she would. But instead, she said something that startled me, and Monroe, too.

"I feel sorry for you. For both of you."

Though her comment prompted laughter in Loo and Hans, Monroe and I both managed to smile her way. I was downright proud of Sue Jan for taking the high road.

Loo sprawled an arm over the back of her chair. "Let me tell you a story. . . . "

Hans leaned over her. "No, Mutter."

Instead she reached back and gave his hand a reassuring pat. "Do not worry, my son. The rice, as they say, is cooked. Besides," she snarled, "no one will live to repeat what I have said."

Now I can't be sure of this, but it sounded to me like Sue Jan and Monroe and I all gulped at the same time. Fear crept up my spine like ants swarming to a picnic.

22

Cold Cashew Chicken

Loo took great pride in her storytelling, measuring each word for weight, meaning, and clarity—which kept us on the edge of our mattress. The only problem was that our bellies started to growl as if someone were playing the xylophone with our hungry and very empty stomachs. We gurgled in succession, one after the other. It was downright spooky. So she stopped, annoyed, and motioned for one of the guards. He disappeared for a few minutes and then returned with three bologna sandwiches on cheap white bread, MoonPies, and Pepsis. Some last meal. Sue Jan did not have a pretty expression on her face, although I did see her glance at the cookie boxes.

Our storyteller began not where she left off, but from the beginning. "Many years ago, two families met by chance or by kismet—fate, if you will. My family followed Sun Yat-sen, leader of the Nationalist Party, who set a goal before him to forge an alliance with the Chinese Communist Party, though it was only in its infant stages at the time." Loo's head bowed down for emphasis or in respect. I couldn't be sure.

Sue Jan yawned loudly.

"The other was the family of my late husband, Fritz. He was sent as part of a German envoy to counsel and advise."

She continued, eyes traveling to each of us like she was giving a toastmaster speech in Denny's. "Sun Yat-sen began to unify a China overrun with warlords. But cancer took him before he could complete his task. That was in—1925—yes. Then a new leader emerged. His name, Chiang Kai-shek."

Loo said the last name with a hard *k*, letting us know that name meant business. "After Chiang assumed leadership, he began what he called a Northern Expedition from Guangzhou to Shanghai. This unified southern China and, more importantly, let the Nation-alists control the Lower Yangzi. Once they got to Shanghai, Chiang launched a massacre of Communist Party members, who fled to the countryside. Some managed to escape his hand. Then, the Nationalist forces received help from German 'advisors' to hunt them down. This is where the story of our family alliance begins."

Loo coughed. With a snap of his finger, Hans ordered one of the guards to return with a cup of tea. She made sweet eyes at her darling son then took a tiny sip of tea and continued her story.

"There, our families met and found that they had much in common. Above all else, however, they shared a love for wealth and power to be gained through the sale of knowledge. So they made an alliance to join together German and Chinese blood, through the bond of arranged marriages. Total trust would be required, trust as is only found in families. Fritz and I were married, then my younger brother, Tan, to Greta, the sister of my husband. Others were married in similar fashion and moved to other locations. We moved to America and began our grand enterprise."

"And what did you do besides open dinky little hole-in-the-wall restaurants?" Sue Jan asked.

Loo handed her teacup to Hans, her tone harsher. "Our restaurants are not 'dinky' as you say. Now, in answer to your second question—we are spies."

I tilted my head. "You sell secrets from Los Alamos! I knew it! That means you're selling American secrets. Putting our country in danger. You—you traitors."

"We prefer to think of ourselves as *traders*," she responded snidely.

Hans cut in with a sly look in his eye. "And it is quite a lucrative trade."

I'd had about all I could stand. Here they were in our little town, spying on our own country, right under our noses—and in Texas of all places.

Moving with the grace of a tiger, Loo stood up next to her son. "And now it is time for us to 'fly without wings,' as we say."

Hans motioned to the guards, who yanked us up from the mattress we were all sitting on.

"What does that mean?" I asked, annoyed by the treatment.

To my surprise and theirs, Monroe answered my question. "It means to disappear without a trace, to vanish suddenly—like wildfire."

Sue Jan mouthed, "How did you know that?"

But before Monroe could answer, the guards came at us. They marched us through a network of tunnels. On the way, I noticed rooms with banks of computers.

Some rooms with military-style cots, others that seemed to be dining areas.

Finally, we were shown to a real prison room with cots. It was dark inside except for a little window covered with black iron bars on the door. They shoved me and Sue Jan onto one cot damp with moisture from the rock walls, and Monroe on the opposite side of the room. Then the guard slammed the door shut. At first everything was pitch black in the room, but then our eyes adjusted and things started to come into focus, in more than one way.

"I hate the dark!" Sue Jan yelled to the guard. "Let there be light. That's in the Bible. I read it." The retreating guard didn't answer, but once outside the door he must have flipped a switch. A tiny bulb, hanging from the ceiling on a single cord, cast a dim light. Not exactly a Charlton Heston moment, but it would have to do. She wiggled out of her bonds like a professional and then helped me.

"Uh, thanks, Sue Jan. They yanked 'em so tight this time my wrists were getting numb."

"We couldn't have known what they were up to," said Monroe. "It wasn't until Bo decided to send you clues that we found out something was going on. The real question is why would Bo turn her back on the life she knows, to expose her family's secrets?"

Sue Jan beamed, or I thought so anyway. It's hard to tell in the dark. "Monroe, I can see why you're such a good lawyer. You really know how to think about things." She undid him next.

He sighed, massaging his wrists. Now I imagined

it was Monroe's turn to beam.

"But I want to know how you knew what that expression meant," she asked.

He harrumphed, probably from having a dry throat, and answered, "They should have had the decency to leave us some water."

"Monroe?"

"Ah. Right." He paused. "When I was in college, I took a lot of specialized courses. I was interested in different cultures and languages. Chinese was one of them. That's all."

"That's pretty impressive, Monroe. You're real smart. I like that."

Sue Jan really meant what she said, too. I could tell.

Maybe we were nervous, being prisoners of spies and all, or weak from being hungry, but we talked and laughed about silly things. Hours passed, and then hunger really kicked in. We tried talking about a whole lot of things—the spies under our noses, Monroe's new job, the beauty shop, the boutique part, our customers, and even how we should redecorate the shop. Of course that last part turned into an argument again, which at least kept us awake.

Sue Jan started getting giddy and lightheaded. Which is when she started telling us the truth about why she was so unhappy.

"You know," she started, "I thought that Hans was my last chance at finding a good-looking man to settle down with. Now I look at him and I don't know what I ever saw in him. The truth is, though, I never had a chance at happiness with Hans, even if he liked me, which he doesn't and never did."

I scooched in closer to her on the damp bunk. "He was never good enough for you, Sue Jan."

She pressed her cheek up next to mine and gave me a butterfly kiss with her eyelashes like when we were kids.

"First off, I gotta admit something to you. I don't hate dogs; I only act like I do. When I was growing up, I always wanted a dog but my aunt wouldn't ever let me have one. She only let me have cats. She's the one who really hated dogs, not me. For years, I've dreamed of owning a pet snoodle."

"A what?" Monroe asked.

"A snoodle. I saw one in a magazine. It's the cutest little dog, a cross between a schnauzer and a poodle, and I *want* one."

I wished that Sue Jan could have fully appreciated my mouth hanging open. You can live with someone, work with 'em, and think you know everything about them, and then suddenly find out you don't. First I find out my best friend's double-jointed and then I find out she not only likes dogs, she wants one of her own. *A snoodle?*

"Lovita. I gotta tell you something else, girl," she added, sniffling. "All these years I've been watching you and this God stuff you're into. I kept expecting you to show me something hypocritical. I wanted you to fail and fall so you could have fun with me and not be such a Christian all the time. But you didn't."

The words got stuck in my throat but I managed to squeak them out. "I—I never knew."

"Just let me finish. I'm the one who took your Bible the other day on the porch. I was reading it. You came in right when I was in the middle of a real good story, so I tucked it in a magazine and took it to my bedroom to finish reading. Right then, I didn't feel like talking to anybody but God. So I took off in my car. Then I got kung pao kidnapped and all."

She took a deep breath. "And before that, when you and Monroe asked me to come to church with you on Sunday, something inside me knew I was supposed to go. It sounds weird, but I was actually excited about going to church. Then, when Monroe got up to go to the altar, I wanted to go right up there with him but I couldn't bring myself to do it."

From across the room, I heard Monroe gasp. "Sue Jan, you mean your heart was moved as well?"

"Yes, Monroe." She let out a sob. "I wanted to follow you."

Monroe sighed. "That would have made me so happy, but even with the way things are now, I'm still happy about it."

I elbowed Sue Jan. "We've got nothing to do and plenty of time on our hands now. Unless they decide to whack us. Do you still feel like answering the call?"

Tears began to flow, streaking down her cheeks. "Answer me this, Lovita, before I do anything like that. Am I going to turn into a Christian zombie or something? Will I still be me? I don't wanna be boring and bland and always walking around saying 'praise the Lord,' like some parrot. Is that gonna happen to me?"

Monroe and I laughed. "No way," I said. "You

can still be you—only a new and improved you. To be honest, you're going to change, but from the inside out. Some things you liked to say or do before won't be as important to you anymore. It's a gradual thing. And for all the things you no longer want to do, there are a thousand more things you can. You'll be at peace with God and with people, and filled with His love."

Monroe added, "And let's not forget eternal life."

I nudged her again. "So how about it?"

She nudged me back with her elbow, a little harder than I would have liked. "I'm ready, Lovita." She squeezed her eyes shut. "Ten, nine, eight, seven. . ."

"What are you doing?" I asked bewildered.

"It's my countdown."

"To what?" I asked.

"Salvation."

Loose Change and
Lychee Nuts

A dull thump sounded outside the door, followed by the clank of the lock turning. At first I thought I was dreaming, then I looked at my light-up watch. It was morning. We had spent the night in Loo's prison. Looking up at the open door, I could make out a female form. Bo.

She motioned to us. "Come now, we must go at once." Her whisper, hoarse and desperate, brought us to our senses fast.

Sue Jan, after rubbing her eyes against her shoulder to wipe the sleep away, was the first to jump off the cot. Monroe and I followed, stumbling out behind her.

Bo had must have escaped from her prison room, wherever that was, and come back to risk her own life and rescue us. That told me a lot about her. But I still didn't know why.

Monroe wiped his brow. "How did you—"

Bo pressed an index finger to her lips. "Shhh. Follow me."

Two guards were slumped next to the door. To my surprise, Bo led us down a series of familiar corridors right back to the kitchen and eased the door shut. Once inside, she and the man at the table met each other's gaze and I began to understand. Bo was in love. There was nothing about *like* on her face. Just a look of pure love, like his.

She grabbed the chains around his ankles and unlocked them in one quick move so they could embrace. Bo wiped tears from her eyes. Having known her all of her nineteen years, I realized at that moment that I had never once seen the girl cry.

"What's your name?" I asked the young man.

He bowed and a curtain of thick dark hair fell over his eyes. "My name is Shaozu."

Sue Jan interrupted. "Does that rhyme with *kazoo*? 'Cause that's the only way I'm gonna remember how to pronounce it."

Shaozu bowed and smiled. "Yes, though I do not know the meaning of that word."

Monroe looked around. "Shouldn't we get out of here now before they find us?"

Bo nodded. "Yes, we are waiting for a few more." She turned to me. "Shaozu is Chinese, smuggled here illegally on a ship through San Francisco. I am ashamed to say that he and his brother were smuggled here by Loo to be slave workers for the family." She looked into his eyes. "But when love grew between us, we realized that our hearts and our lives beat as one." Perspiration on her brow, she looked up at the wall clock. "There is no time to explain any further. We must leave now."

But just as she said it, the door turned on its hinges. We all froze in our tracks. In walked Tan and Greta, Bo's parents. The door swished shut behind them.

Tan's eyes looked sad, and Greta's hazel eyes were

tinged with red as if she had been crying. Bo ran forward to hug them.

"I'm so glad you made it. Thank you, Mother and Father, for releasing me. I could not have escaped without your help. You have saved all of our lives because of your bravery, but you must come with us now before it is too late."

Tan embraced her lovely face in his worn hands. "Bo, you are named for Bo Le, the horse judge. It is *bole shi ma*, a talent scout, a person who can discover talented people and know their worth. Have you indeed found worth in this man?"

Bo and Shaozu exchanged looks. "Yes, Father. He is a good man and I love him."

Tan seemed pleased. "Your mother and I want you to have a better life. This is no way for you to live, in secrecy and lies. You deserve the right to live a normal life, to marry and raise a family."

To the point of tears again, Bo asked, "But you know what will happen if you stay here?"

"Daughter, do not worry over us," he answered, solemn voiced. "We made our choice many years ago. Though we have no joy in this work, please permit us to have hope and joy in knowing that you and the young man that you love so dearly are free of this wicked pact."

Shaozu stepped forward and stood at Bo's side. He bowed before Tan and Greta. "Sir, I want to tell you from where I sat as a prisoner, that there is hope and a way to break free of the ties that bind you. It is through faith."

Monroe, Sue Jan, and I stood transfixed. *Shaozu a Christian?*

He continued with sincere respect. "Sir, you must have faith in God that He will deliver you out of these impossible circumstances."

Tan shook his head. "No, Shaozu and Bo, my beautiful one, it is too late for us. Much too late. Go to your freedom and live a good life. We rejoice with you."

The door swung open as if kicked. Six guards with guns charged through and trained their weapons on each of us. Then Loo and Hans entered.

A halfway grin on her face, she gestured with her arm. "I see that you were right, my son. We have gathered a nest of traitors for ourselves today." She walked to stand triumphantly before Tan and Greta. "You betrayed all of us for one."

Normally silent, Greta spoke up, eyes blazing with grief and tears. "She is our daughter, you wretched woman."

Tan, reaching an arm around her shoulders, comforted and quieted her.

Bo spoke, her young face glowing with righteous indignation. "I am happy to be named a traitor to this wicked enterprise, a breaker of a pact I did not make, and would never choose to make. Shaozu and I love each other." She moved closer to him. Her eyes flashed the heat of repressed anger. "He taught me a better way to live. An honest way to do business, to have family integrity, and to be a friend. This is how I choose to live my life."

The two guards on either side of her responded by

cuffing her hands behind her with plastic bonds. Then they did the same to her parents and Shaozu.

Loo laughed. "You have made the wrong choice and will die with him." She looked around. "In fact, you shall all share the same fate. But not just yet." She motioned to the guards. "Bind them as well."

Sue Jan muttered to herself at first, then her voice grew louder. "Oh great, we're right back where we started."

"Be quiet!" Hans yelled. He waved his gun in small circles in the air. "You talk too much, you round little pork chop."

Sue Jan flushed with anger. "Just who do you think you are, talking to me that way?"

He ticktocked with his index finger. "Such a harsh response. May I remind you of your lowly status? After all, you are a condemned prisoner, with much emphasis on *condemned*." He drew close to her face and continued. "I have wanted to tell you, *Miz Sue Jan*," he mocked, "for the longest time and most certainly before you die, that you are not as witty or charming as you imagine yourself to be. In fact, you have all the charm of a feral cat."

He threw in one last word, for good measure, but it clearly hit both Sue Jan and I where it hurt. "Nor are you beautiful. You and your porcine friend are like two walking, wiggling tubs of lard."

He seemed to spit the last sentence out. It was clear that Hans Han had anger issues. And what was with the ticktock move? He relied on that tired motion way too much.

Loo called to Hans, and he veered away from Sue

Jan, much to her relief. He signaled the other guards, who pushed us all into a corner of the kitchen and made us sit down on the cold, hard floor. While two guards stayed with us, three others went out into the corridor and returned with dollies. They began to travel back and forth from the storeroom, through the kitchen, out into the corridor and beyond, their dollies piled high with boxes and boxes—of cookies. Like a Girl Scout Cookie Jamboree. The remaining guard took something out of a black pouch.

Something with a timer attached to it. . .a bomb?

The others noticed it, too. An explosive device in a room is hard to miss. Kind of like an elephant in a room—hard to ignore.

Deep in conversation on a cell phone, Loo seemed concerned. She whispered something into Hans's ear, and he shot out of the room. For some reason, they were all in a hurry.

I worked up a dose-full of courage, fueled by the sight of the bomb, and raised my voice so Loo would hear what I had to say. "So that's how they do it."

She lifted her chin. "How we do—what?"

I lifted my chin to match hers. "That's how you get the secrets out—through the cookies. I'll wager a bet it's the lucky numbers at the bottom of the fortune. The ones with purple ink are special cookies, the ones with the secrets people buy."

Loo smiled but it quivered on the edges as if she was nervous. That important phone call must have been bad news. She motioned to one of the guards, who drew me away from the others and pointed his weapon at me. Among the prisoners, a hushed silence fell. "Where is it?"

I responded with more of the same. Silence.

"Where is the recipe?"

The guard clicked the weapon.

Hans returned to whisper something into Loo's ear, which prompted a heated exchange in German, I think. Sounded like German, anyway. Mixed with a bit of Chinese. Ger-nese.

"Step up the pace!" Hans ordered. In English. Frazzled.

One of the guards emerged excited, carrying an open box out of the stockroom and chattering something. Sue Jan's face blanched white at the sight of it. He showed it to Hans and Loo then opened it to reveal the crumble of fortunes, wrappers, and crumbs. The guard pointed at Sue Jan.

Looked like the pressure was off of me temporarily.

"Oh n–no," Sue Jan stuttered and rose to her feet. The rest of the prisoners nervously stood up with her.

Hans jumped at Sue Jan and yelled to her face, his own contorted in fury, "You fat fool! Look what you've done!" He shoved the empty box at her.

Loo joined in. "Who eats an entire box of cookies? What a pig you are. You—you belong on a farm or in a circus."

The guards began to laugh at Loo's cruel remarks.

Instead of snapping back, Sue Jan convulsed in tears. But when Hans raised his hand to strike her, the fireworks began. While they'd been busy hauling cookies, Monroe, with Sue Jan's help, had worked his hands free from the plastic cuffs. And when Hans threatened Sue Jan, Monroe's fist landed hard and square on Hans Han's perfect nose. And to my surprise, the muscular Hans went down like a thermometer in a blizzard.

Loo sank to the floor by his side. "Hans!"

Right then, the door kicked open for the second time. Six men I recognized from the khakis crowd, but outfitted now like a SWAT team, fanned out with guns trained on the bad guys.

"Put the weapons down, now!"

The guards hesitated, but with Hans on the ground and Loo on the floor next to him, they obeyed.

"Now put your hands above your head. Slowly," a SWAT team member said. "Do it now!"

Loo and Hans stood and, along with the guards, obeyed, holding their hands up in the air like they all knew the answer to a question. This time it was their turn to feel the cuffs. The SWAT team bound their hands and led them out. Then I heard a familiar sound. The clomp of boots in the corridor. Clint Greech walked in.

"You doing okay, Lovita? Sue Jan? Monroe?"

I nodded. So did Monroe. But Sue Jan was still sobbing in Monroe's arms. Monroe kissed the top of her head and lifted her chin with tender care. Sue Jan's face was streaked with tears and mascara.

She turned her head to the side. "Don't look at me, Monroe. I'll bet I look like a rabid raccoon, a big fat rabid raccoon. I feel dirty and ugly and embarrassed for you to see me like this."

The leader of the SWAT team yelled, "Everybody—

out! Bomb squad's on the way!"

As if in another world, Monroe's palms reached for her face once again. "You are the most beautiful woman in the whole wide world. Lovita was right about Hans not being fit to deserve you. I don't feel like I'm deserving of you either."

Tears began to fill Sue Jan's eyes *again*.

His face gentle, he spoke to her. "Sue Jan, I've always loved you, but I love you more now than ever before." Then Monroe sank to one knee.

The room suddenly fell silent. I think we were all holding our breath, spies and SWAT team, FBI or CIA or whatever they were, alike. Sue Jan stared wide-eyed at Monroe.

"Sue Jan—" he paused to wipe a tear from his eye. "Would you marry me?"

Now I don't know what got to her, the lack of food, the recent threat of Hans Han, or the question Sue Jan had waited over half her life to hear, but she fainted—right into the arms of her future husband.

The SWAT team leader swatted the air. "*Now!*"

Lo Mein Leader

Once we were above ground and down the street from the warehouse, Clint offered to cut our ties with small wire cutters he took from the pocket of his coat. But Sue Jan and Monroe were already free. I was the only one he could help. Bo, Shaozu, Tan, and Greta would remain in handcuffs with the others for now, at least until things were sorted out. Hopefully, the federal agents' cuffs were comfier than the plastic ones we'd had on, and not as easy to get out of.

They moved us to a pool hall down the street temporarily, but Sue Jan was too punch drunk from the marriage proposal to marvel at the seventies disco ball covered in cobwebs and grease stalactites, hanging from the ceiling.

"Clint, why didn't you answer your cell phone? I left messages."

"Sorry about that, Lovita. I did get the messages eventually. I was on a flight from New Mexico when you first called and then lost reception temporarily when you called again. I got your messages soon enough, though. Your friend in the diner caught up with me and gave me the envelope you left with her."

I smiled. Good old Callie. I knew I could depend on her.

Hungry, exhausted, and stressed, I was starting to feel the effects of the last twenty-four hours. But I still had questions and too much curiosity for my own good. "What about the Bentley police, Clint? Did you ever contact them and find out why they never came to investigate?"

He stared down at his boots for a moment, and then he looked up. "Lovita, I'm real sorry about that but I couldn't tell you. We had to keep the local police out of it. They knew about the operation to some extent and totally cooperated with us."

"Well that's a relief. I was starting to feel like a second-class citizen!"

He took his hat off and stroked the top of his head. "To be honest, we've had our eyes on you the whole time. The men on the street. . ."

"You mean the workers? The electrician, too?"

He nodded a yes slowly, a slight smile on his face. "When Sue Jan disappeared, we decided to tighten security on you and Monroe."

Loo, Hans, and the goon guards were in a corner of the room, off to themselves. Unlike us, they deserved to be handcuffed and sitting in a corner! Clint started to talk, but he couldn't seem to get anyone's attention at first. It was hard to hear with all the different agents on walkie-talkies or cells and people going in and out the door to the outside. I listened to their conversations—or snippets of conversations at least, and heard they were going through to the secret door. I guess there was a lot of other evidence to gather. I was relieved to hear them say the bomb squad had carried the bomb outside. Thankfully, the timer hadn't even been set yet. Praise God!

Sue Jan and Monroe, cooing at each other since he'd asked for her hand, were in a different world, so there was no sense trying to talk to them. Bo and Shaozu were starry-eyed, too, even though they both faced prison and/or deportment. Tan and Greta wept in each other's arms from shame or relief. Or both. Clint turned to me.

"When I received that fortune cookie message, I knew something was up. There was always something suspicious to me about the way your father died." Clint stopped to lightly scratch the tops of his ears. "Anyway, I found out there was a big investigation already underway, and I managed to join up with them by pulling a few strings and calling in some favors."

I never knew Clint had such strong feelings about my daddy's death. There had never been any hint of suspicion as far as I knew, and if Mama had any, other than the jealous kind, she'd certainly kept them to herself.

"And the information in the envelope—is that all the evidence you need? The recipe and fortune connection?"

"Yes, Lovita. It should be all the evidence we need."

"And there's a letter I found that Daddy sent to Mama where he talked a little bit about the investigation."

"Your mother did show me that letter, right after your father died. But it didn't give any vital information to help us out. We've known for a long time there was a spy ring operating in this country, somehow involving

Chinese restaurants, but their plan was perfect. Genius, in fact. No one could figure out how they did it. Until you ladies got on the case." He grinned.

A blaze of thought flashed through my mind. "Daddy mentioned there were matchbooks from the restaurants he visited. He—he was probably investigating as much as eating!" I latched onto his wrist. "The matchbooks! I remember now! They're in the fallout shelter. In a big glass jar in the locker."

He patted my hand. "Good work, Lovita. You're your—"

"Father's daughter," I finished.

When I looked up, everyone was listening. My eyes were wide as canning lids. So were Clint's.

"Please excuse me," Bo cut in. "MizLovita," she bowed her head, "I must ask your forgiveness—"

Perplexed, I touched her quivering shoulder. "I forgive you."

Bo bowed again. Not an easy thing to do in handcuffs. "MizLovita, please listen to me. I need to confess something to you."

This time Clint spoke. "Bo, I have to tell you if you plan to go on with this, you should only speak in the presence of a lawyer."

Her eyes shifted in thought, then they seemed to light up. She pointed at Monroe. "He's a lawyer. Monroe, would you represent me, at least for now?"

Monroe looked from her to Clint to me and then to Sue Jan, who blinked a positive. Our visual cues seemed to make things okay. He raked a hand through his hair. "Yes, Bo, I'll represent you for now. I don't know if I can later, though, since I'm involved in this." He came and stood beside her and made sure her Miranda rights were read.

"Now, Bo," I said, "before you say a thing, I need to know a couple of things. Were you the one following us and did you kidnap Sue Jan?"

She shook her silken hair. "Yes, I followed you, MizLovita, hoping you would give the message to the police, but then I discovered the federal agents were also trailing after you. It was difficult for me to both follow you and avoid them. I could not be the one to reveal the secret. I feared for my parents and Shaozu and his brother."

She reached up, hands limited by the cuffs, and lightly pushed a swatch of hair away from her face. "As for MizSueJan, Loo had her taken because she knew you would come for your friend. Hans and Loo were aware of my betrayal to the family when he found the kung pao recipe with the codes on it in your kitchen." She breathed hard. "They forced me to cooperate with them, or my parents and Shaozu. . ."

"Then Loo sent the threatening message—with instructions to meet at the Cut 'n Strut," I finished, touching my chin in thought. This was a lot to process. "Then," I asked, "Bo, when Monroe and I were at the warehouse, looking for Sue Jan, you knew we would follow you?"

"Yes, I hoped so."

I pulled and twirled at my hair, nervous. "But. . .if the recipe hadn't slipped out of Hans's shirt. . ."

She shrugged. "I would have made sure you had

another piece of evidence."

"Were you the one in the kitchen, too, that day I got the fortune about my daddy's death?"

"No, Shaozu's brother worked with Hans in the kitchen at Chun's that day. He was forced to work as a cook and waiter for Loo. A slave as well. If he refused, his brother would have been killed. I convinced him to help me, though, and he was eager to do so. My plan was our only chance of escape from this way of life."

"How did he make sure I would be the one to get that cookie?"

"Although you and MizSueJan usually have separate checks, I was not willing to take the chance that you would receive the wrong bill. I told him to place a red pen on the bill tray with your cookie," she answered softly.

Bo continued. "MizLovita, the message in the fortune cookie about your father. . ."

"Yes?" I whispered, my heart skipping.

She looked from Monroe to Shaozu, then to me. "They are not true. Your father was not murdered."

"*What?*" My lip started trembling out of control.

"I designed that message to attract you and your father's friend, Mr. Greech, to get your attention. I heard you talk about your father in the shop when you and Sue Jan spoke of your childhood and family." She continued, eyes misty. "One learns much from listening, and I learned much about you and MizSueJan. I know that MizSueJan likes eating and to discover new makeup techniques. And you, MizLovita, like to solve puzzles and you do not give up until you solve them. I've often wondered what it would have been like to have a normal childhood, instead of one filled with fear and dread that we would be discovered and captured."

Hands bound and uncomfortable, Bo turned awkwardly to glance at her parents across the room. "My parents tried to help me live a normal life, but spies are not able to do so."

A flood of relief filled me as I panted out, "Then my father died of natural causes?"

She looked away for a second, a black curtain of hair waterfalling to the side. "I hesitate to tell you this, but I must, MizLovita. I believe that your father, Mr. Clark W. Horton, died from an allergic reaction to MSG. You must speak with my father, Tan, about it."

I stood useless as a dead tree, until Clint brought Tan over to us. "Is—is it true, Tan?"

He stepped forward. "Yes, MizLovita, I believe it is true. Your father, much as you are now, was quite fond of Asian cuisine. He would eat at Cheng's and Chun's, four days a week. Interestingly, his favorite dish was shrimp egg foo yong. As is yours." He bowed his head. "However, I began to notice that after your father would eat meals with us, he suffered with indigestion and his skin would redden. Over the course of weeks, I noticed that after his meal he would have breathing difficulties and perspire much, as well. At that time, not much was known about the effects of MSG on some people. We used it grandly in our dishes. I am not a doctor, but in my humble opinion, your father died of an allergic reaction."

Clint spoke up. "But the morning he died—"

"He was eating leftover Chinese food," I interrupted, feeling odd and blank inside. "I thought he was having eggs and bacon, but now I remember. H–he was e–eating l–leftovers from the—the night before." I began to cry. "Mama and me, we were having a regular breakfast, but Daddy loved—"

"Leftover Chinese food," said Clint, a morose expression on his face.

Sue Jan wrapped her arms around me, but the tears couldn't get past the state of numbness. I was relieved and in shock at the same time. And sad, too. If all this was true, then my daddy died for nothing.

A mocking laugh caught our attention across the room, now quiet with revelation. Loo pushed forward, her perfect hair now disheveled. An agent followed closely. "So, you think that Clark Horton died of natural causes?" She threw her head back. "If you believe that, you are all fools."

Clint stepped forward. "Just what do you mean?"

A wry smile escaped her lips. "Because, Mr. Greech, I killed him."

"Stop, Mutter!" Hans stomped, frustrated. Two agents on either side restrained him.

One of the agents read Loo her Mirandas, all to the tune of Hans's protests.

Sue Jan tapped Monroe on the arm. "What's he telling her?"

Monroe whispered back, "Her Mirandas."

Then Sue Jan elbowed me and in her version of a whisper, passed it on. "Ita, that agent's reading Loo her

Carmen Mirandas, whatever that is."

Hans's protests got louder and louder. Finally, Loo stared him to silence.

I felt faint; my knees buckled. Sue Jan tightened her arms around me, and Monroe came up from behind to help hold me up.

Bo lowered her head. "I did not think it possible, but I am further ashamed of my family."

Loo focused on me. "Were you aware that your father and my late husband were friends?"

The shock that washed over my face seemed to satisfy her intent.

"It was perplexing to me. Fritz and I seemed quite suited to one another. But for some reason, he began to seek out your father's advice on matters of religion. In spite of my warnings to avoid close associations with others, he pursued this 'friendship.' " Loo swayed a bit, then she asked for a chair. The agent brought her one.

"They often shared lunch and spoke of God. Fritz, in turn, became softhearted and weak."

Clint added, "And he shared something, as well, didn't he?"

Loo offered a half nod. "Our family secret. He could no longer bear it on his conscience. I recognized early on that Mr. Horton was a danger to us and that he exhibited a peculiar reaction to our spice. We know from observation and experience that some cannot tolerate it. So, I began to add more and more to the dishes he ordered. And his reactions became more pronounced."

"Am I hearing this right? You killed my daddy with

MSG?" I felt the blood boil under my skin. How could she do a thing like that to my father? He was a good man, and she took him away from me and Mama.

"Yes," she sneered. "He had to be dealt with. He was asking too many questions and lurking around. Our organization, our way of life, was in danger due to his investigation. Someone had to take the lead."

Suspicious, Clint interrupted. "What about Fritz? Didn't *he* take that lead? Or did you kill your husband, too?"

"No. No." Hans convulsed violently in defense of his mother. The agents held his shoulders, and he bucked hard against them.

"Yes." Loo closed her eyes to say it, clearly bothered by it even after all these years. "And I have always regretted it. Though it was an arranged marriage, I—I loved him. But he and I could not agree. " She looked at the wall beyond us. "He was willing to sacrifice all that we had worked to achieve. I could not allow that. Our own lives would be forfeit to those we answer to. Our son, Hans, too."

In shock at this betrayal, Hans hung his head low and stared at the floor.

Clint focused on her. "Ma'am, did you ever attempt to poison Miss Lovita Mae Horton?"

She pursed her lips, most of her bile and bravado gone. "I saw the same qualities in her as in her father. Word of her message traveled to my ears and I knew she would be curious. I wondered if she, too, would be susceptible to MSG." A triumphant smile escaped. "To that end, I tested her vulnerability recently, but did not discover with certainty whether or not she is like her father. If she is, like a poisonous snake, I would have begun to bite her a bit at a time, as I did her father, until in time she, too, would have succumbed."

Clint circled his hands around my shoulders. "You were feeling a little sick at Cheng's the other night. Remember?"

Dazed at the thought that someone would try to take my life, I managed a slight bob of my head.

In a gruff voice he called to the agents and pointed to Loo. "Get her out of here! And set up a med-check for Lovita M. Horton. ASAP!"

Clint's earnest green eyes soothed my troubled spirit. He drew me aside. "Lovita, one important thing I've learned over the years is to trust God. He knows what He's doing. Your father gave his life in the line of duty. He also led a lost man to Christ. Trying to figure out why things happen is a whole lot harder than just letting go of the reins."

I sobbed into his arms and he soothed me, just like Daddy would have.

A couple of men approached from the outside door. Clint introduced them. "These are agents McPheal and Donovan." The men lifted their sunglasses for a brief second. I recognized their faces, but the eyes confirmed it. The two "hotties" from Cheng's.

Clint went on. "To make a long story short, this German-and-Chinese family decided to operate a little spy ring here in the US. They've been at it for a long, long time."

"For China?" I asked, curious.

Donovan answered, "For anyone willing to pay their price."

McPheal stepped forward. "Spies in the Los Alamos National Laboratory were stealing top secret information, coding it into Chinese recipes, and then sending those to various Chinese restaurants. Their contacts in the restaurants deciphered the codes, assigned new ones, and transferred that information via the lucky numbers typically found on the bottom line of fortune cookie fortunes."

I let out a low whistle. "Clever. I've always wondered about those. I mean, what does anyone use those for anyway?"

McPheal folded his hands together. "I don't know. Maybe gamblers or bingo enthusiasts. I've never seen any use in them—until now."

Clint held up the envelope I'd given Callie. "With this and other evidence they already collected, we'll be able to break up this little Szechwan spy ring for good."

"Don't forget about the matchbooks."

"And the matchbooks." He turned to the agents. "They're in Lovita's house."

"In the fallout shelter."

Donovan coughed. "The what?"

"Fallout shelter. It's a long story," I added.

Clint bobbed his head. "There might even be some evidence jotted down on them. Clark Horton was a meticulous investigator, but he was clever, too. He told me he had some hard evidence on these people, but none of that surfaced after he died." He stroked his chin. "We'll see what rises to the surface now. "

"Stirring the pot." For once, my mouth was moving along with my brain.

"What?" he asked.

I laughed. "I'm not crazy. It's something I was thinking about before."

McPheal, eyes full of mischief, pulled a fortune cookie out of his pocket and threw it to me. "Before you were taken prisoner in a Chinese fortune cookie factory?"

Chuckles and snorts came out of me, but Clint and Donovan held it together for the sake of *day-corum*. I could tell by their eyes, though, that they were laughing inside.

McPheal had to add, "You'll never live that one down, Lovita."

I scrunched my nose at him. "Well, back to what I was saying. Seems like such a long time ago now, but I was thinking about cooking. You know, when you stir the pot, all the scum rises to the surface so you can skim it off."

"I've got a spoon ready to go at it," said McPheal.

Clint shook his head, still fighting back laughter. "They staked out some suspects and found that they had one thing in common—their travels from San Francisco to Los Alamos to New York. They frequented Chinese restaurants in small towns along the route."

"That's why you went to New Mexico Sunday after church?" I asked.

"Yup. We did it, Lovita."

Clint and I high-fived one another.

Sue Jan high-dived into the conversation in her

usual way. "What do you mean, 'we'? I'm the one who led all of you to the German-Chinese mafia. Without me, you wouldn't have solved a thing. If I hadn't sacrificed my thighs and eaten that whole big box of fortune cookies, these spies would still be sitting pretty, stealing secrets and sending 'em out with the lunch special. I'm the hero!"

"And?" I asked, knowing full well where she was going with it.

She twirled a stray strand of hair. "What I would like to know is—is there some kind of reward for this?"

"Sue Jan!" I snorted.

"Shush, Ita."

Clint removed his hat and scratched the top of his head, then he put it back on. "I—I reckon we could give you a medal or something, Sue Jan. There's no reward money."

Hans yelled from across the room, hands bound in front, agents bookended on either side, holding onto his shoulders. "What are you saying, you brainless fool?"

The agents were already marching the others out to a van. With a flick of his wrist, Clint beckoned them over. Chin held high, Hans stuck out his lip like a two-year-old who didn't get his way. He continued spouting off at Sue Jan, the current object of his scorn. "You have the physique of a hippopotamus and the brain of a mosquito."

What a nerd!

It was too much for Monroe, who stepped forward to take a swing at Hans, but Sue Jan pulled him back.

"I–I'll pray for you, Hans." She looked at Monroe. "Correction. That's what *my fiancé and I* are gonna do *together* for you. We're gonna pray." She hooked her arm through Monroe's and planted a kiss on his lips. Monroe was completely mesmerized.

But Hans Han flinched suddenly from the surprising effect of a handy gallon of mustard going down the neck of his custom-made suit. Much to everyone's surprise, I threw the container down and patted the back of his suit to grind it in deeper. "Even a mosquito gets a pat on the back when he's doing his job," I said, winking at Sue Jan.

HAIR FOREVER

A voluminous pink satin ribbon, suspended from two iron hitching posts, surrounded the new and improved shop. Hudson's hand embraced mine as we stood next to Sue Jan and Monroe, with a crowd of well-wishers—customers, friends, and family. Though I was already walking on cloud nine, it was time for the official ribbon-cutting ceremony for Crown of Glory—formerly Lovita's Cut 'n Strut.

"Thanks for being here with me," I said, looking up at Hudson. "It makes this opening ceremony all the more special."

He squeezed my hand and looked down at me. "Lovita, I wouldn't be anywhere else on this earth, but here today."

On the outside I was calm and cool at his incredible answer. On the inside, a Hershey bar on the pavement in August's noonday sun in Wachita, Texas. There was just no getting around it. Hudson was dreamy.

Turns out that I am allergic to MSG. Just like Daddy was. Lab tests and doctors confirmed it. I can still eat Chinese food, though. I just have to make sure there's no MSG or any other letters of the alphabet near my dinner plate.

The spy ring was mainly busted up on account of

Bo. Tan and Greta helped her. And Shaozu, of course. And his brother. Last I heard, Hans Han is a prison chef, serving up bologna sandwiches on white bread. And in the women's big house, Loo is in charge of the prison "loo," keeping it sparkly clean and all. I guess with a name like Loo, you could see that one coming. I wonder if there are Tiger Balm bars at all the sinks.

After we recovered from all the excitement of spies, federal agents, revelations, generations, salvations, and the fact that the only two Chinese restaurants in town were now shut down, Sue Jan and I sat down together and had a long talk about what we wanted out of our careers and lives.

I'll admit, I had to do a lot of praying and soul-searching at first. After all, Mama passed the shop on to *me*. But in the end, I had peace in my heart about making the change. Sue Jan's like a sister to me. So I asked her to become a full partner in the business. Really, not that much was going to change. I would still manage the boutique part, except that I had expanded the clothing line to double what it was before and added a ton more accessories. Sue Jan would run the beauty shop part, including nails, makeup, and even adding massage therapy. We were a little sad about Bo not being able to come back and work for us, though, but Jolene agreed to take her place—temporarily.

"What do you say, Lovita, is it time to cut that big ole ribbon, girlfriend?" Dressed in a matching pink satin suit, her brown hair now with blond highlights in an updo, accented by an antique rose swiped from Tan and Greta's rose garden, she looked good. Sue Jan and

Monroe had agreed to keep an eye on their house and take care of the garden until Bo was officially released from the investigation. Because she agreed to cooperate, coupled with the fact that she was already working to expose the spy ring, they weren't going to press charges.

Bo and Shaozu crept up behind Sue Jan—who turned around, screamed in surprise, and let out a whoop. I knew they were coming. Clint told me. He vouched for them with the authorities, which I know was instrumental in getting them released. The biggest problem, though, was that Shaozu was gonna be sent back to China since he was here illegally.

What a change. Instead of wearing the rags Loo gave him to wear, Shaozu wore a white polo shirt and beige pants. I noticed a small antique cross around his neck, too.

"MizLovita and MizSueJan"—Bo beamed, holding up her left hand to reveal a miniature diamond—"I'm married." She jumped up and down. Shaozu added a wide grin to the mix. I guess when a girl is truly in love, the diamond in the wedding ring could be microscopic for all she cares. Except in Sue Jan's case.

"Bo," I exclaimed, "I believe you're as happy as a clam!"

Sue Jan piped in. "I never understood that saying, Lovita. I mean, what do clams have to be happy about? The only time I've ever seen one is when it's minced up in a soup or sauce, gittin' ready to be eaten." She held up a pink-clawed hand to Bo. "Don't be happy as a clam, Bo—just be happy, that's all."

Bo smiled and looked into Shaozu's eyes. "I will."

The two had been married in a civil ceremony by the same judge that let Bo go. Clint had even served as one of the witnesses. Now he stepped forward to join our group, tipped his hat, offered Shaozu a hearty handshake, then planted a kiss on Bo's cheek.

"Let's do it, Lovita," Sue Jan urged, impatient. "It's gittin' hot out here. Pretty soon all my makeup'll melt off."

Sue Jan and I stepped up to the ribbon, placed glittery plastic tiaras on our heads, and picked up the biggest pair of scissors I'd ever seen. The two of us smiled, holding the scissors, and looked back for Jolene, chomping her gum and waiting with a camera. Then we cut the ribbon to Crown of Glory and invited everyone in town to come inside for punch and cookies.

If only I had a dollar for every *ooh* and *ahh* I heard when people stepped through the door, the renovation would have paid for itself. The truth is, though, insurance barely paid for half the shop to be redone. Unbeknownst to me and Sue Jan, Monroe did us the kindest and sneakiest deed of his life. The day after our little trip to Bentley, he went back to Jolene and ordered all the fancy beauty stations and equipment I had been drooling over. I guess Monroe paid more attention to things than I thought. When he told us what he did, Sue Jan liked to fall over the table where we were having lunch. And I was speechless. I couldn't imagine anybody doing something so nice for us and spending so much money for nothing in return. But Monroe told us, "Without your help, Lovita, I wouldn't have the love of my life sitting here next to me. You helped both of us to get right with God, too. I'm happy to help out."

The look of the new place was downright outrageous. Sue Jan went wild over the new stuff. Light pink marble station tables, bordered in black, with drawers for everything and holsters for all the tools of the trade I had bought previously. And those pink-and-chrome leather chairs. Yessss, real pink leather; not that Naugahyde stuff. From pink cows, according to Sue Jan.

After Monroe and Hudson put up some new drywall, Sue Jan and I tried our hand at Venetian plaster on the walls. We probably got more of it on the tops of our heads than on the walls at first, but we soon got the hang of it—the palest of pink, glossy with a wax overcoat and smooth as river rock.

For artwork, we decided to enlist the local high school art class. They agreed to rotate the pictures every semester so we would always have fresh art on our walls. Plus maybe the kids and their parents would visit the shop to look at their framed creations and then get their hair done or shop in the boutique. Sue Jan and I were using our heads this time, but more important than that, we were using our hearts, too. Since Sue Jan decided to become a Christian, we had become closer and more in agreement about things than ever before. Except for the fact that she still thinks the shop needs a disco ball.

Funny, we both thought we were close and that it just wasn't possible to be closer friends. The difference now is that we're like sisters. And that's good. Real good.

We did the floors in old oak planks from an abandoned farmhouse. Monroe and Hudson worked evenings and weekends, fixing 'em up for us. And the floors looked wonderful. Monroe says they have a patina that only comes with age. They're smooth, too. I guess a lot of feet walked over those boards through the years.

It was Hudson's idea to save a few wide planks from the farmhouse kitchen and use them for the sales counters in the shop and boutique. They looked beautiful, too.

A handbell rang out. "Excuse me, everyone. Purr-aise the Lord!"

"'Scuse her. C'mon now, everyone listen *por favor*."

Hazel and Inez stood on a couple of step stools. They were dressed in pink and black in honor of the new shop colors, and each of them had tucked a pink zinnia behind her ear for a festive touch.

"We just want to say a few words about our girls, Lovita and Sue Jan," said Hazel proudly.

Inez nodded, "*Si*, we do." Her pink lipstick some-how seemed even more pink and frosty today.

Everyone clapped.

"Most of you know that Bessie Mae Horton was our close friend. We loved her and had some good times," she said as she rocked her head at Inez.

"Si, we did. . .good times," Inez agreed.

Hazel went on, accenting every word with a flip of her wrist or twitch of a finger. "And we were here, full of pride when she gave this shop to Lovita and had a dedication ceremony much like today for Lovita's Cut 'n Strut. She said a prayer over Lovita that day, that all her works would prosper, and that girl has done well to the glory of God."

Clap, clap, clap.

"Si—yes indeed." Inez nodded.

"A little while ago, we would have told Lovita not to make Sue Jan her business partner because she would have been unequally yoked," Hazel continued.

Clap, clap, clap.

I wondered why people were clapping at that, but I blew it off.

"But then we got to praying." Inez shook her head as if agreeing with herself.

"And Sue Jan answered with her heart. Purr-aise the Lord!" Hazel yelled out.

Inez spoke up. "And we prayed for husbands for them, too. Godly husbands, and God is good. Now Sue Jan is getting married soon, too."

While people were still clapping, Hazel added, "And let's not forget Lovita. She and our missionary boy have been like two peas in a pod lately." Hazel held up a hand to her ear. "Wait, do you hear something?"

Confused, people looked left and right at each other and toward the door.

"I think I hear. I think it's—it's wedding bells. Lovita's next!"

My face flushed red with embarrassment, but Hudson seemed to enjoy it.

Sue Jan signaled me to follow her toward the stockroom. We made our pardons to Hudson and Monroe and everyone in the crowd along the way who wanted to talk.

I closed the door behind me. Sue Jan was already leaning, elbows down, on the worktable. She held a hand up to one ear like she was straining to hear something.

"What?" I looked around then pressed my ear against the door. "What is it?"

"Do you hear that?" she asked.

I paused. "No, all I hear is a lot of people talking and eating and having a good time in our brand-new splendiferous shop."

"Listen. You sure you don't hear it?"

"No. I don't know what you're—"

She pretended to swoon on the table. "Wedding bells!"

I lunged at her and chased her around the table a few times before we collapsed laughing.

"S—Sue J—Jan, when she—she said that. Th—th—that was probably *the* most embarrassing moment of my life."

She hunched her shoulders forward, still giggling. "Who cares? Hudson sure didn't seem to care. In fact, I think he liked when she said it." Sue Jan punctuated her pronouncement with a wink.

"Stop," I begged. "You're puttin' the cart before the horse. I—I hardly know him."

"What's to think about? Hudson's a godly, gorgeous guy, and it's obvious to everyone the man's crazy in love with you, Lovita."

Good a time as any to change the subject. I pulled a wrapped package out of a brown bag off a shelf. "Here, Suey, I got you a little something."

Her expression softened, and she reached out slowly for the purple and lavender polka-dot-wrapped present. She ran her hand over the giant grosgrain bow. "Oh Ita, you shouldn't have. I—I didn't get you anything. Didn't even cross my mind. I'm sorry."

"Will you quit yapping and open the thing?" I put my hands on my hips.

Tongue hanging out the side of her mouth, she set to ripping and shredding the paper to the bare white box underneath. She ran a finger under each side to sever the cellophane tape and opened the lid. Then she charged in through the pristine tissue wrap and pulled out the aqua dress I knew she loved.

Her eyes wide as kiwis, she stood up before the floor-to-ceiling mirror on the wall of the stockroom, holding the dress in front of her body. "Ohhhh. Ohhhh. Ohh. Ita, you shouldn't have." She turned back with a smile. "But I'm glad you did."

"Thanks. Oh, but there's one more thing in that box."

She blinked, handed me the dress, and dug through the tissue once more. This time she pulled out a sparkly tiara. Sue Jan held it up to the light, and the crystal beads twinkled like a fancy chandelier. "I can't thank you enough, girlfriend. The outfit is bee-you-tiful. Perfect for a fa-fa-she-she event, like, for instance—a going away outfit after I git hitched and become *Mrs.* Monroe Madsen." She pursed her lips like she was voguing for the camera.

I laughed as I folded the dress and wrapped it back in the tissue paper, but as I maneuvered between giggles to put it back in the box, I knocked the tiara off the worktable.

"I'll git it." Sue Jan bent over to pick it up and stayed down a few seconds longer. When she popped up, she held the tiara in one hand and a small box of fortune cookies in the other. "Look what I found."

I scrunched my nose. "Are those left over from one of our carryouts?"

"Guess so." She threw one to me. "Open one. You go first, Lovita."

I shook my head back and forth. "No way. I—I don't wanna look at another fortune cookie for a while. And they're probably stale anyway."

She frowned. "Don't go psycho on me, Ita. You and I don't have time for a fortune cookie phobia. We have a wedding to plan. Who knows? Maybe *two*. . ."

Frustrated, I looked up at the ceiling and rolled my eyes back down. "Oh, all right." I reached for the box and snatched one in my hand.

Sue Jan put hers down on the table and motioned for me to do the same. "On the count of three. One—two—three."

Smash. Our hands came down on the cookies, and the fragments filled the wrappers. I fished mine out first.

"A handsome stranger will enter your life."

I whistled. "Guess that one's on the money."

Sue Jan held up her fortune. "With the one you got, I cain't hardly wait to read mine." Silent for a moment, she drew closer to it, as if she couldn't see, or believe what she saw. At first, her mouth moved, but no sound came out. Then in a whisper, she tried.

"What? I can't hear what you said."

"*Help.*"

"What?"

"'Help.'" Her voiced strained at the seams.

"Help, what?" I asked.

"*Help, I'm being held prisoner in a Chinese fortune cookie factory.*"

The room was silent, except for the noise outside. I pointed at her. Sue Jan pointed at me. When the howls of laughter finally came out, the noise brought Monroe, Hudson, and half the partygoers to *our* door.

"Aha, aha-ha-ha. Ahhhhh-ha, aha-a-hahaha."

"Fortune c—coo-key f-fac-tree. Oh, Ita. Aaaaah-ha, ahahahahahha."

Doubled over, I looked up and shouted. "Looks like somebody else is sending out an SOS!"

As the message passed from person to person, the sound of laughter grew. But when the fortune reached Bo and Shaozu, they seemed to get the biggest kick out of it of all. The two of them sat on the floor next to each other, delirious, tears running down their faces from laughing so hard. Bo said they were gonna frame that fortune and hang it on the wall of their own restaurant someday, as a reminder of how they got started. She told us they decided they're gonna name their new Chinese restaurant Wok of Ages. I really like that name. It sounds dee-lishus. And I hope they git to it soon, because Wachita can't go on too long without good Chinese food.

The party went on till way after dusk. As we stood outside in the cool evening air, waving at the last of the guests, Monroe next to Sue Jan, and Hudson by my side, Sue Jan and I leaned forward to peek at one another and smile. And we didn't have to say a word. Our prayers were answered, our dreams fulfilled.

"Look!" Monroe pointed at the night sky. "A shooting star."

I sighed as a warm, wonderful feeling of contentment wrapped around my heart. Good old Wachita. Like a comfortable pair of shoes. It's that kind of place.

HANS HAN'S NOT-SO-ROMANTIC RECIPE FOR KUNG PAO CHICKEN

Packs an emotional punch!

One important thing to consider before you make this recipe at home, especially for a date, is to make sure he's worth slaving over a hot wok. Make this yummy recipe for someone you love!

Souse Sauce:

1 pound chicken, boneless, skinless, uncooked. Chop into 1-inch squares.

2 tablespoons oyster sauce (I've always wondered how they make this stuff.)

2 tablespoons sherry or rice wine

1 teaspoon cornstarch

Spices is Nices:

4 tablespoons cooking oil

½ cup roasted peanuts

1 teaspoon finely chopped gingerroot

2 teaspoons chili paste

¼ teaspoon crushed red pepper flakes

1 teaspoon crushed garlic

Vegetables:

1 clove garlic, crushed

2 green bell peppers (or 1 green and 1 red), cut into ½-inch squares

1 (5 ounce) can sliced bamboo shoots, drained

¼ cup chopped white onion

3 stalks celery, sliced thin

4 shallots, sliced into ½-inch pieces, including tops

Secret ingredient: ½ teaspoon of finely diced jalapeño. Just a word of warning. . .don't rub your eyes after slicing jalapeños. I learned the hard way!

Sauce:

2 tablespoons soy sauce

2 tablespoons rice vinegar

4 tablespoons chicken broth

1 teaspoon garlic powder

1 teaspoon sugar

1 teaspoon cornstarch

1 teaspoon sesame oil

2 teaspoons hoisin sauce

Measure and karate chop all ingredients before cooking. Mix **Souse Sauce** ingredients in a bowl, stir well, and marinate for 30 minutes. Mix **Sauce** ingredients in another bowl and set aside. Heat wok or large frying pan until water drops dance around. Add cooking oil to wok and heat for a few seconds. Add remaining **Spice** ingredients to wok and stir-fry for 30 seconds. Add **Chicken Souse Sauce** to wok and stir-fry for 4 minutes until chicken is cooked through. Add **Vegetables** to wok and stir-fry for 2–3 minutes. Stir **Sauce** and add to wok, and boil for about 1 minute until sauce thickens. Stir to coat other ingredients. Salt and pepper to taste. Serve immediately with steamed or fried rice (my favorite).

LOVITA'S YUMMY FRIED CHICKEN RECIPE

Serves six (or one *very* hungry person)

A small jug of buttermilk
2 teaspoons cayenne pepper (It's red and hot.
   Do not sample!)
2 fryer chickens, each cut into 8 pieces
2 cups regular flour
Salt and pepper
½ teaspoon Lawry's seasoning salt
Vegetable oil or shortening for frying
½ cup butter

Mix buttermilk and cayenne pepper together and dunk each piece of chicken real good. Cover with plastic wrap. Refrigerate at least 6 hours or overnight to make the chicken soooo tender and yummy!

In a brown paper bag, combine the flour with the remaining dry ingredients. One at a time, place the chicken pieces in the bag and give 'em a good shake. Then put the coated pieces on a clean plate.

In a cast-iron frying pan, turn up the heat to about 350 degrees on a good hunk of vegetable lard. Drop a small cube of bread in the oil, and if it browns in about one minute, it's ready!

Using tongs, add chicken one piece at a time, being careful to not overcrowd the pan. Don't move the chicken for about 5 minutes or until the coating looks firm and deep golden. Cook the pieces 8–20 minutes (depending on size), turning them periodically until crispy brown and cooked through.

Drain on a paper-lined baking sheet and serve (any temperature).

This is a real hit at church picnics!

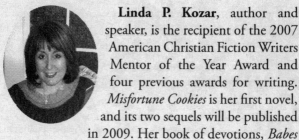

Linda P. Kozar, author and speaker, is the recipient of the 2007 American Christian Fiction Writers Mentor of the Year Award and four previous awards for writing. *Misfortune Cookies* is her first novel, and its two sequels will be published in 2009. Her book of devotions, *Babes with a Beatitude*, will also be released in 2009. Linda works part-time at Lone Star Community College, Montgomery Campus as a Staff Facilitator for *The Global Pen*, a magazine by and for ESOL students. She is the cofounder and director of Words for the Journey Christian Writers Guild—Southeast Texas Region, in The Woodlands, Texas. She will assume a post as president of a new chapter of the American Christian Fiction Writers in The Woodlands, "Writers on the Storm," in July of 2009. She has been a Bible study teacher for fourteen years and currently coleads a women's Bible study group, "Babes with a Beatitude," at WoodsEdge Community Church in addition to managing a ministry Web site by that name. She and her husband, Michael, married for 19 years, have two lovely teen daughters, Katie and Lauren.

You may correspond with this author by writing:
Linda P. Kozar
Author Relations
PO Box 721
Uhrichsville, OH 44683